DISNEY

ZOOTOPIA

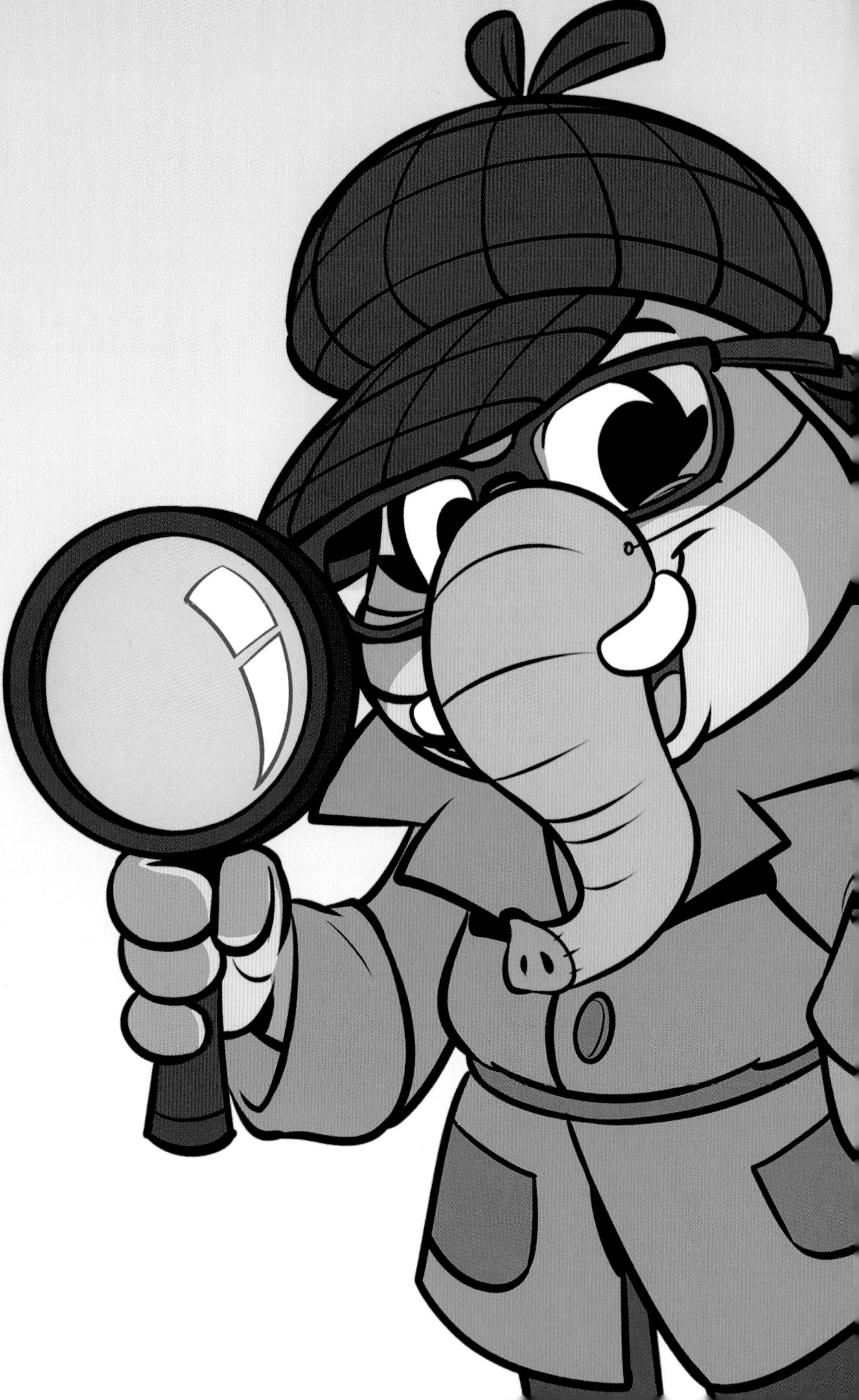

Disney
ZOOTOPIA

A HARD DAY'S WORK

Script by
Jimmy Gownley

Art by
Leandro Ricardo da Silva

Colors by
Wes Dzioba

Lettering by
Chris Dickey

Dark Horse Books

JUDY HOPPS

Judy is an energetic, clever, and big-hearted bunny from the rural town of Bunnyburrow. She loves helping others and will lend a paw at any chance she gets.

NICK WILDE

Nick is a sweet, friendly, and mischievous fox from the big city of Zootopia. He has a natural ability to make others smile and laugh.

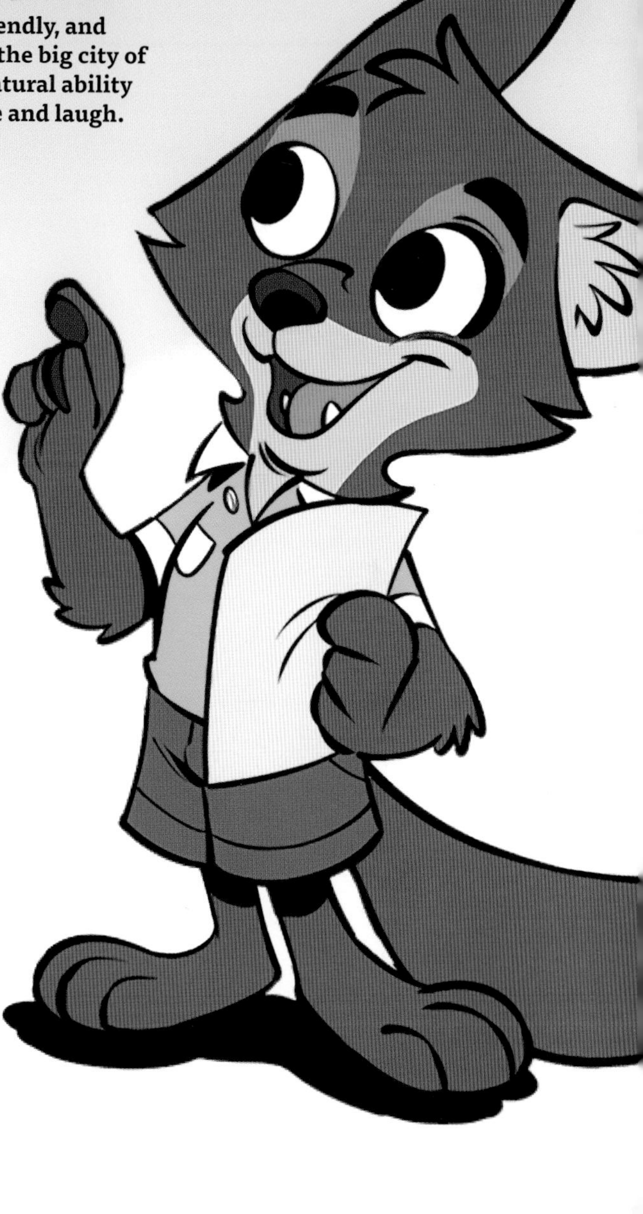

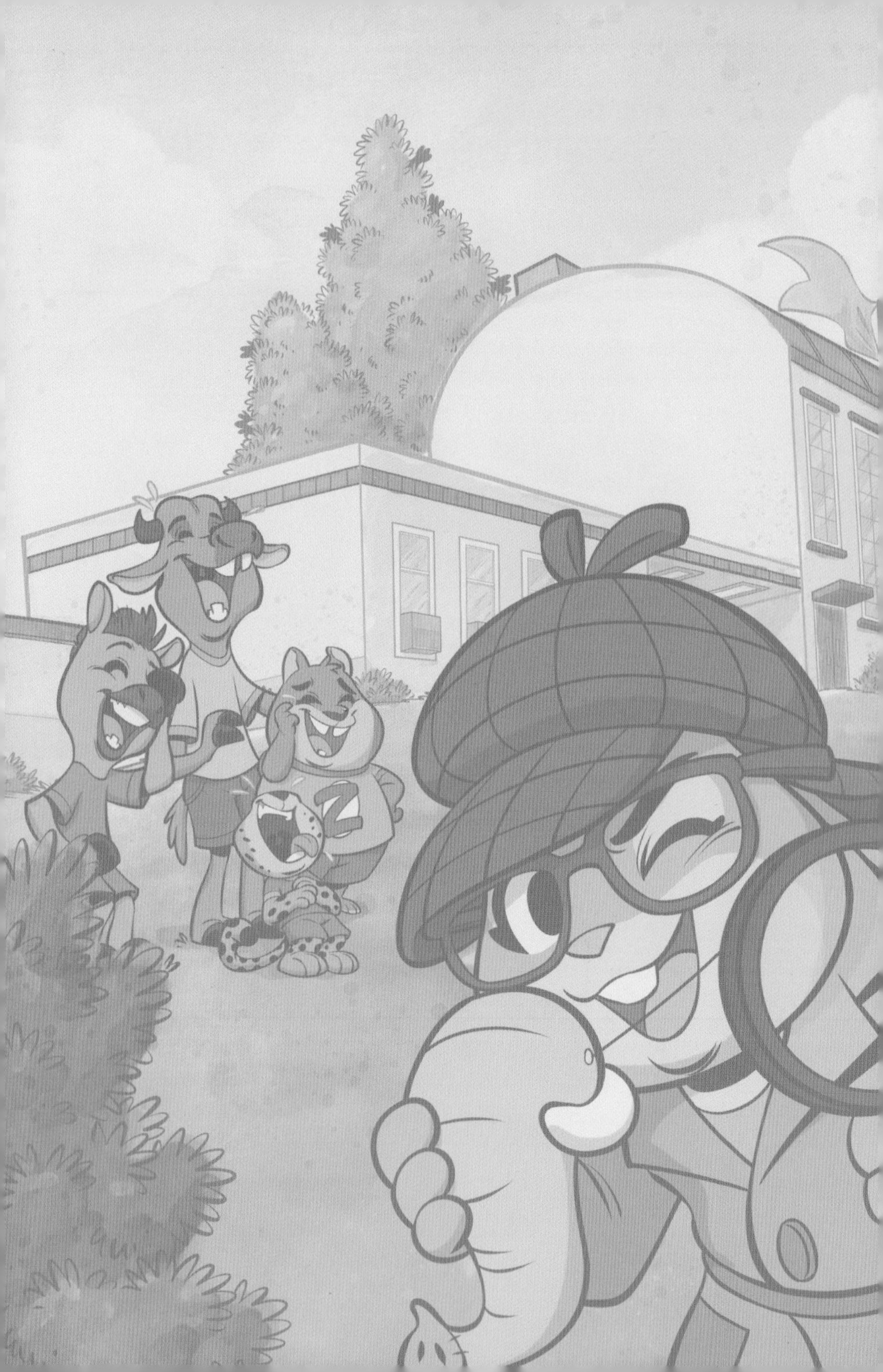

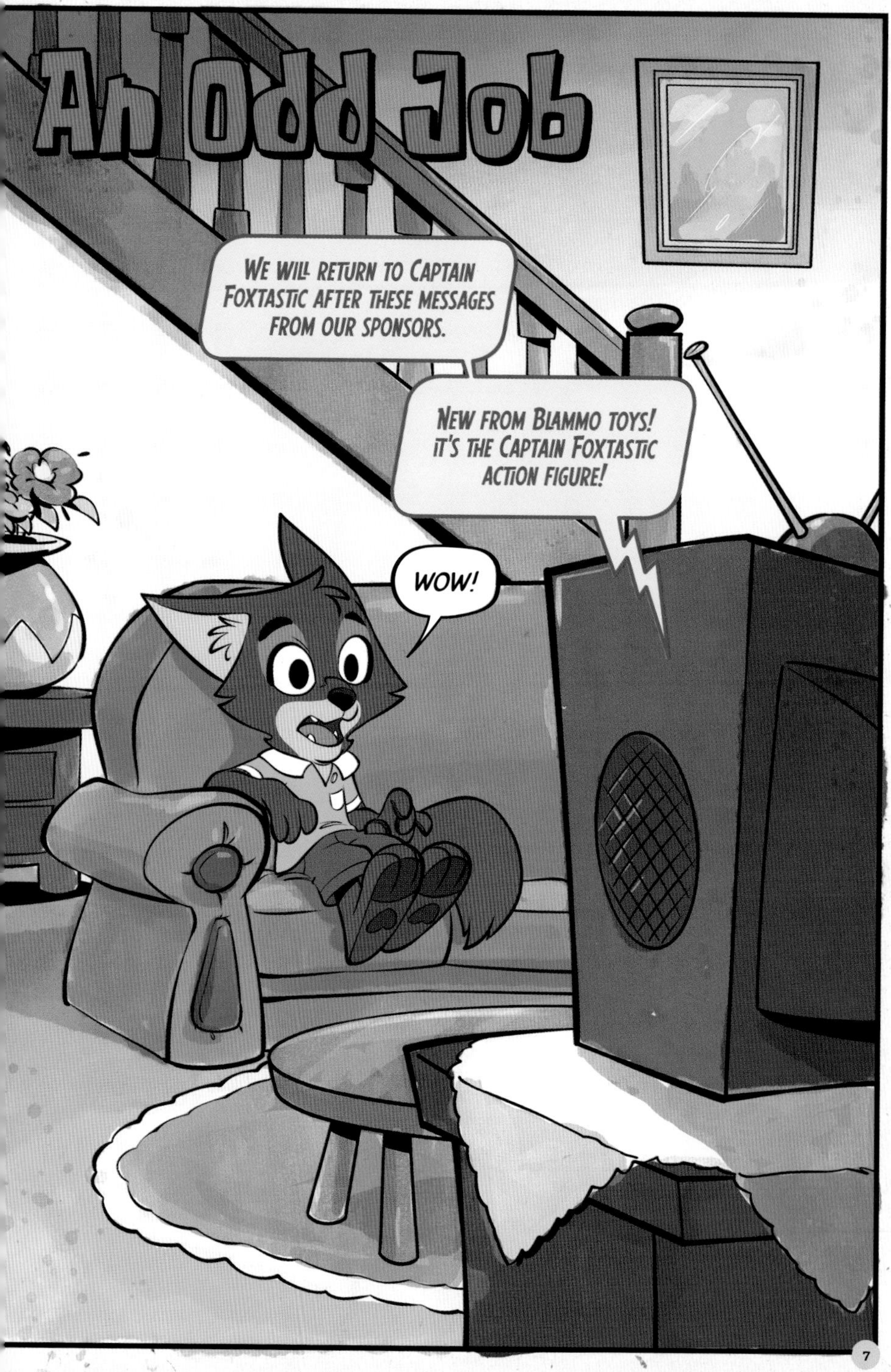
An Odd Job
WE WILL RETURN TO CAPTAIN FOXTASTIC AFTER THESE MESSAGES FROM OUR SPONSORS.
NEW FROM BLAMMO TOYS! IT'S THE CAPTAIN FOXTASTIC ACTION FIGURE!
WOW!

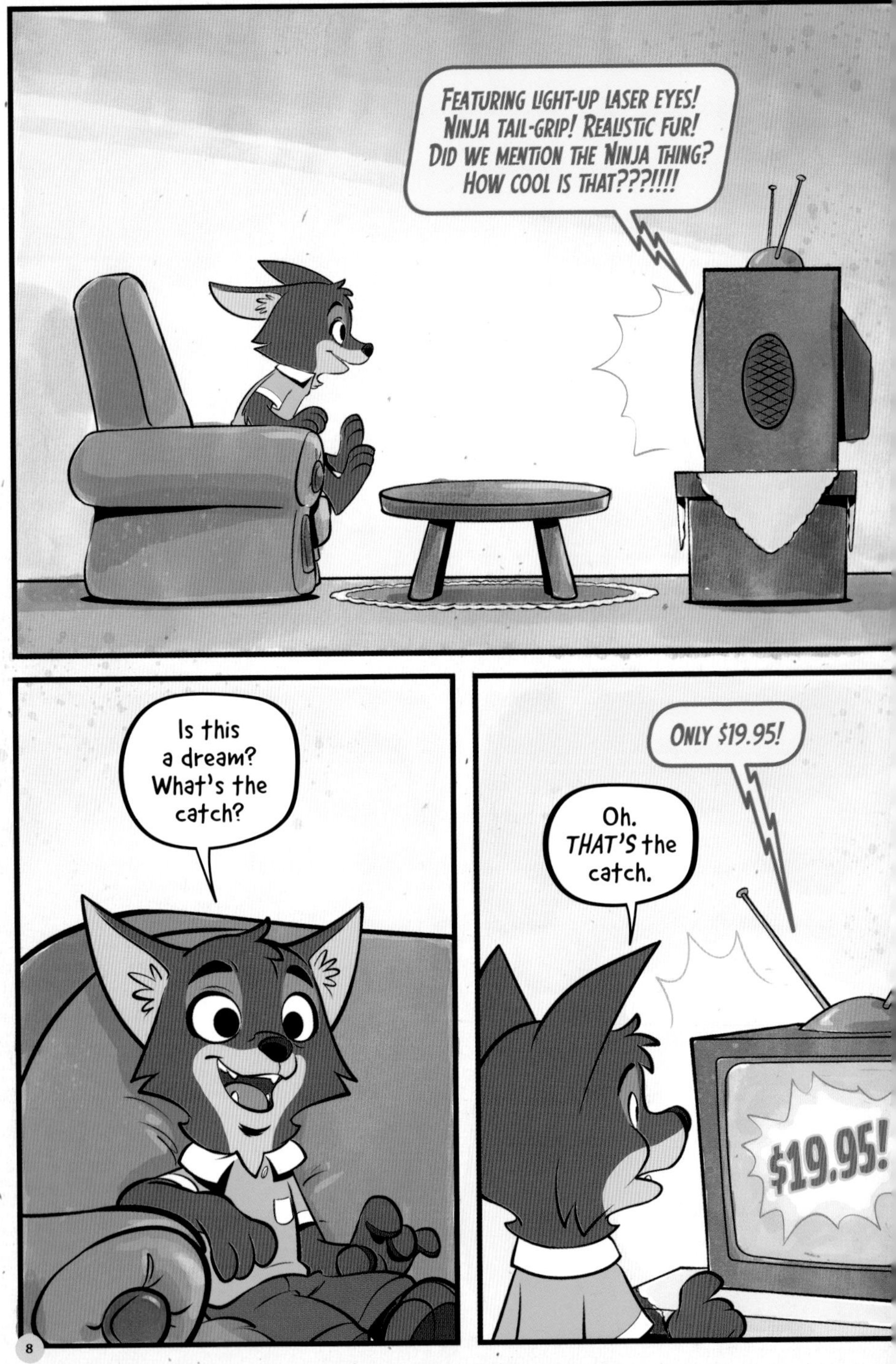
FEATURING LIGHT-UP LASER EYES! NINJA TAIL-GRIP! REALISTIC FUR! DID WE MENTION THE NINJA THING? HOW COOL IS THAT???!!!!
Is this a dream? What's the catch?
ONLY $19.95!
Oh. THAT'S the catch.
$19.95!

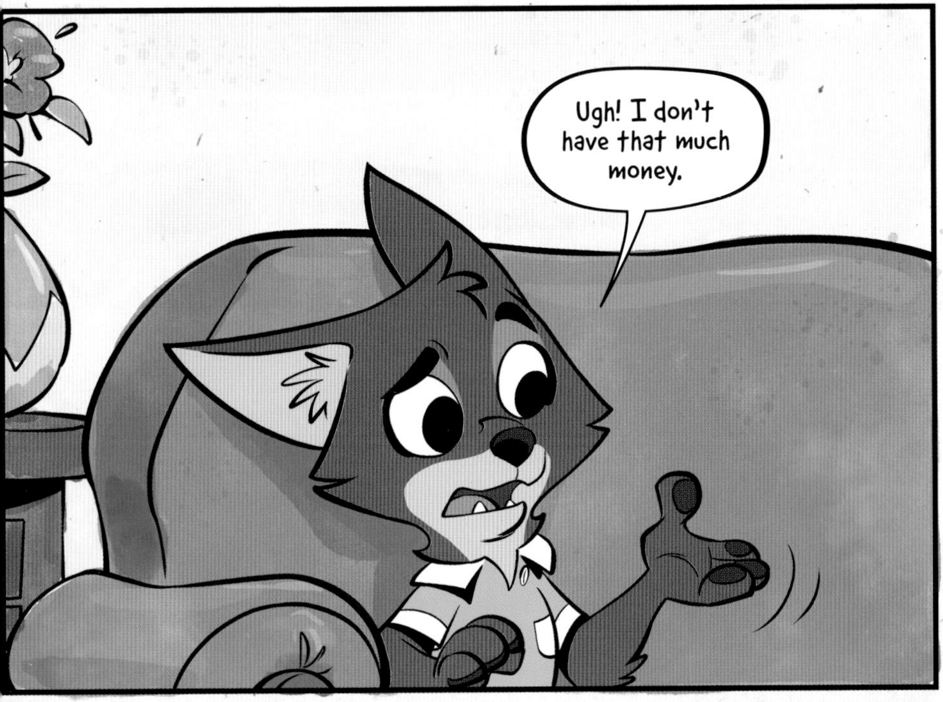
Ugh! I don't have that much money.

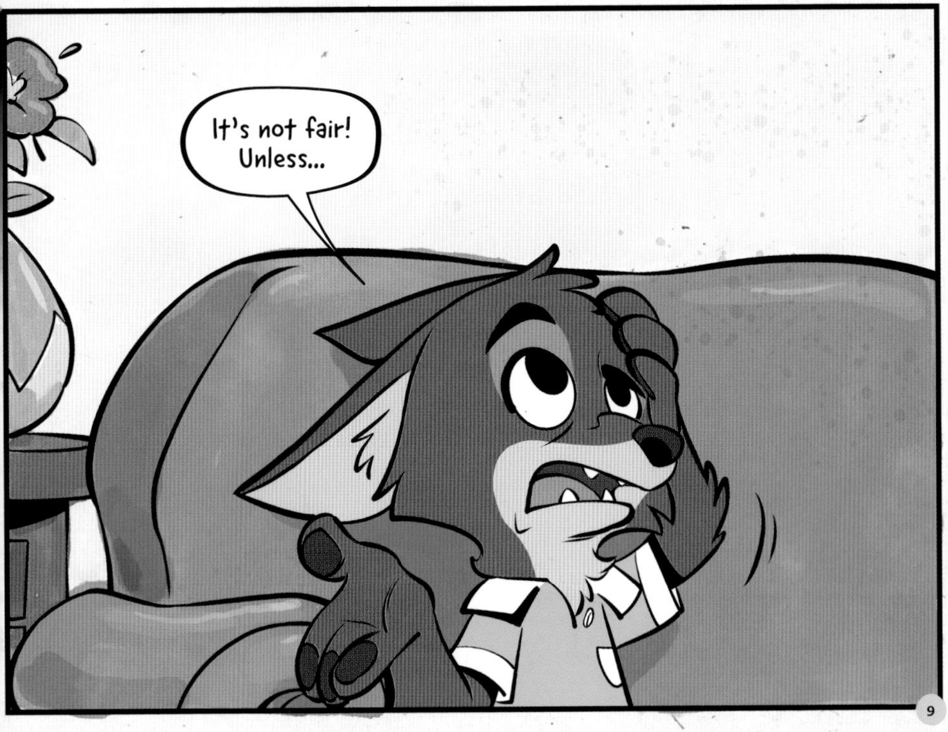
It's not fair! Unless...

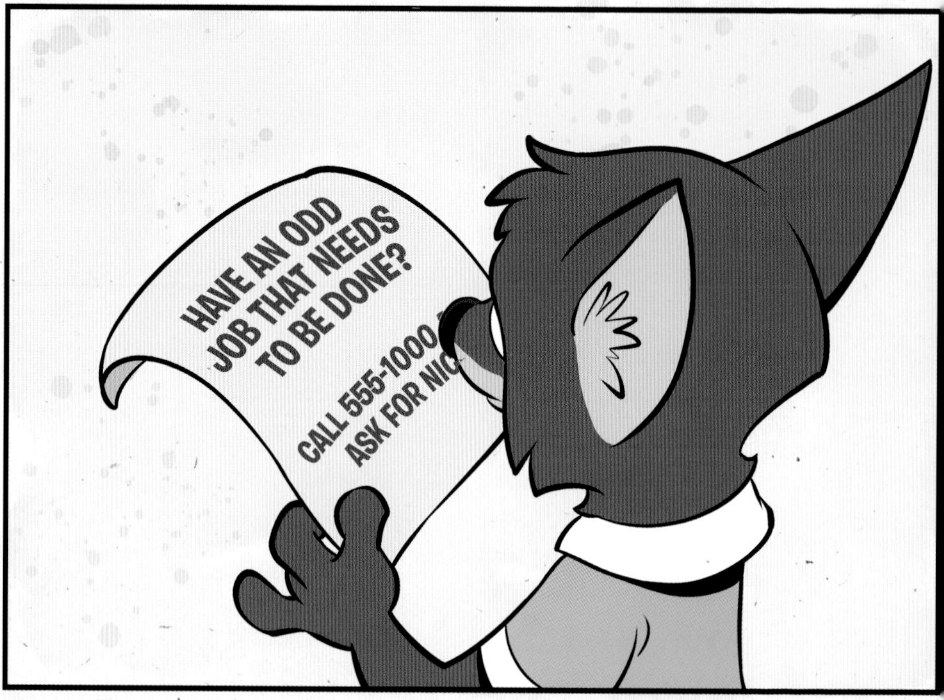
HAVE AN ODD JOB THAT NEEDS TO BE DONE?
CALL 555-1000
ASK FOR NIC

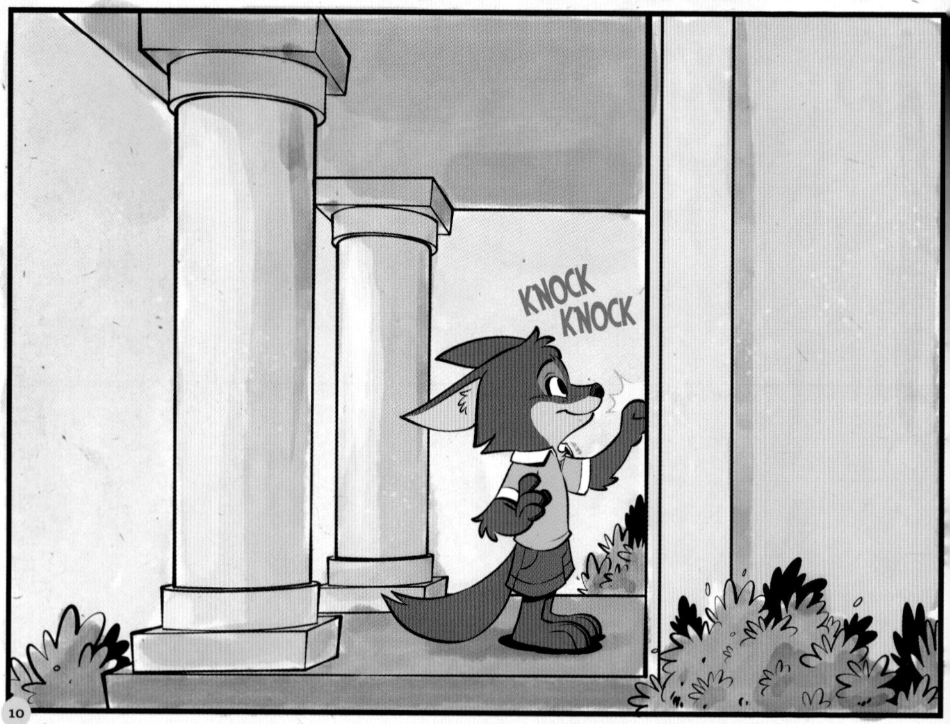
KNOCK KNOCK

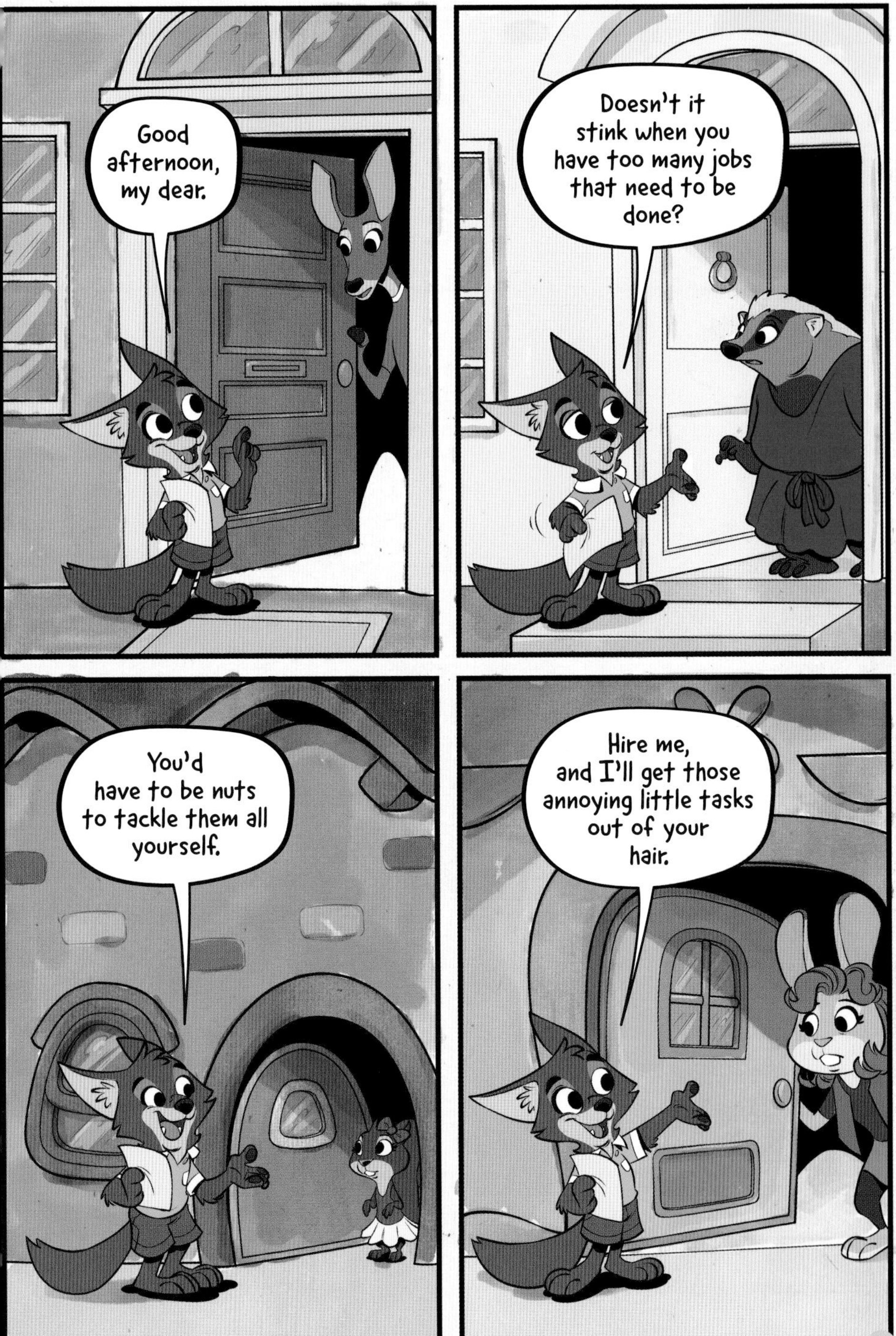
Good afternoon, my dear.
Doesn't it stink when you have too many jobs that need to be done?
You'd have to be nuts to tackle them all yourself.
Hire me, and I'll get those annoying little tasks out of your hair.

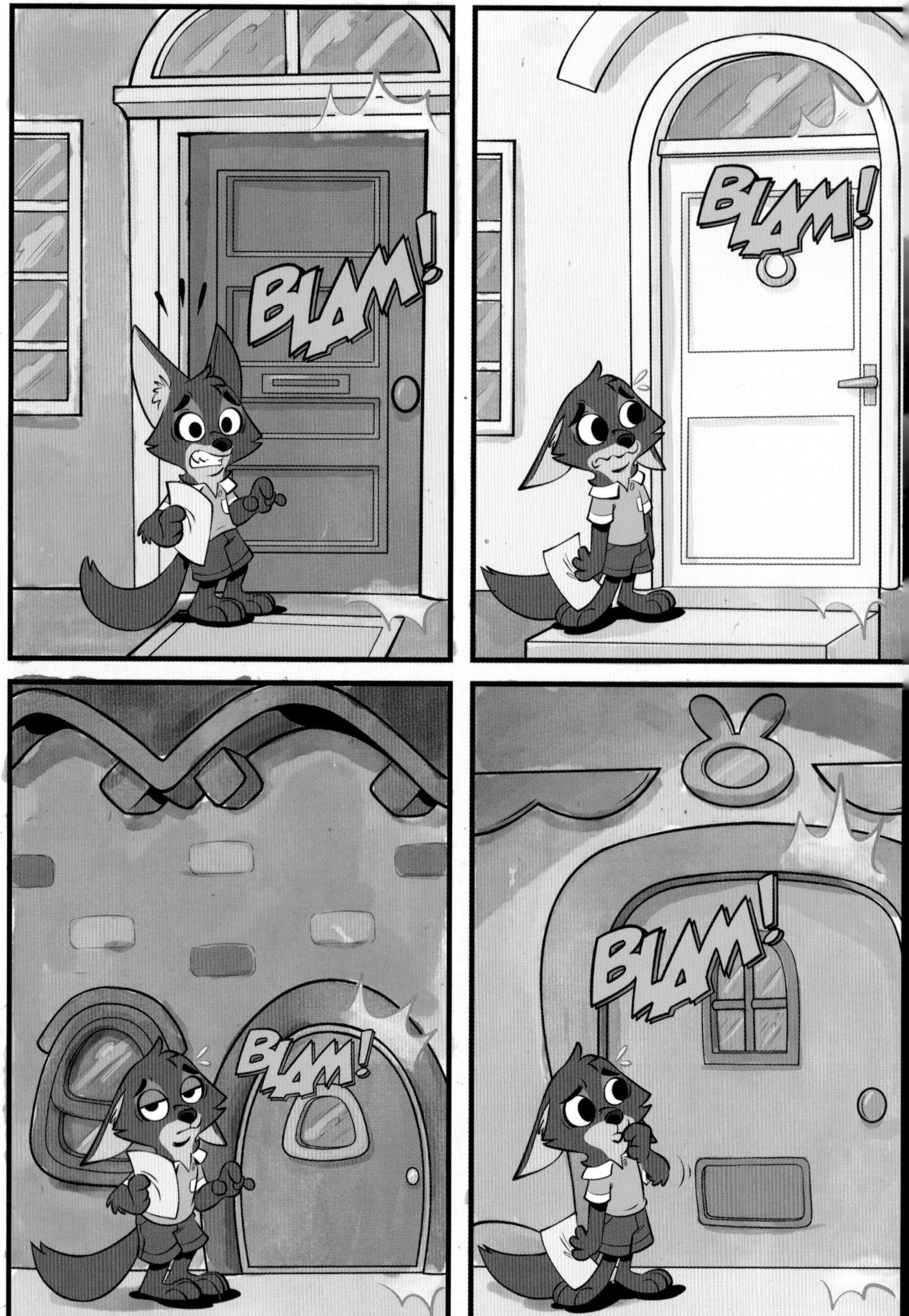
BLAM!
BLAM!
BLAM!
BLAM!

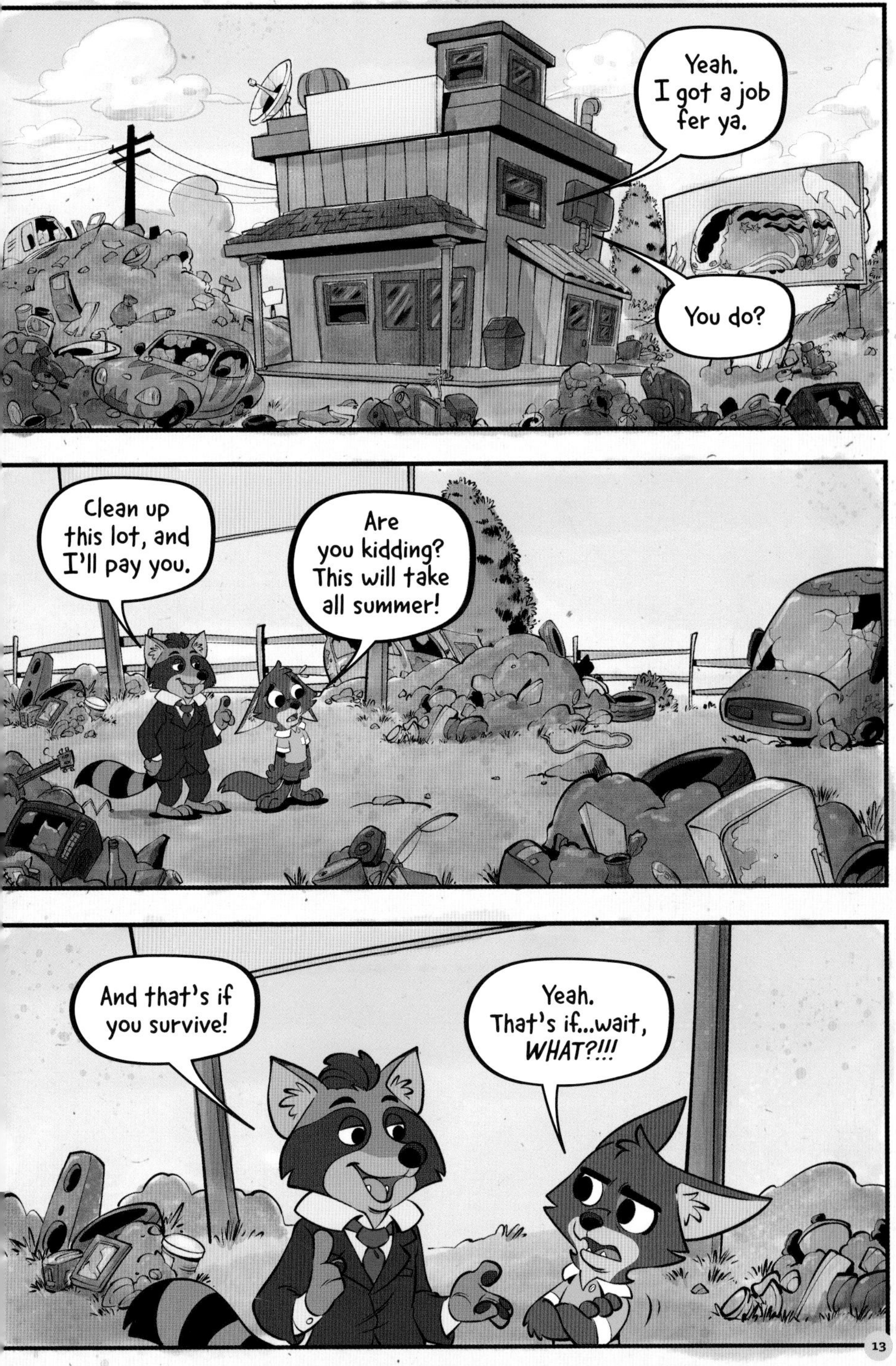
Yeah. I got a job fer ya.
You do?
Clean up this lot, and I'll pay you.
Are you kidding? This will take all summer!
And that's if you survive!
Yeah. That's if...wait, *WHAT?!!!*

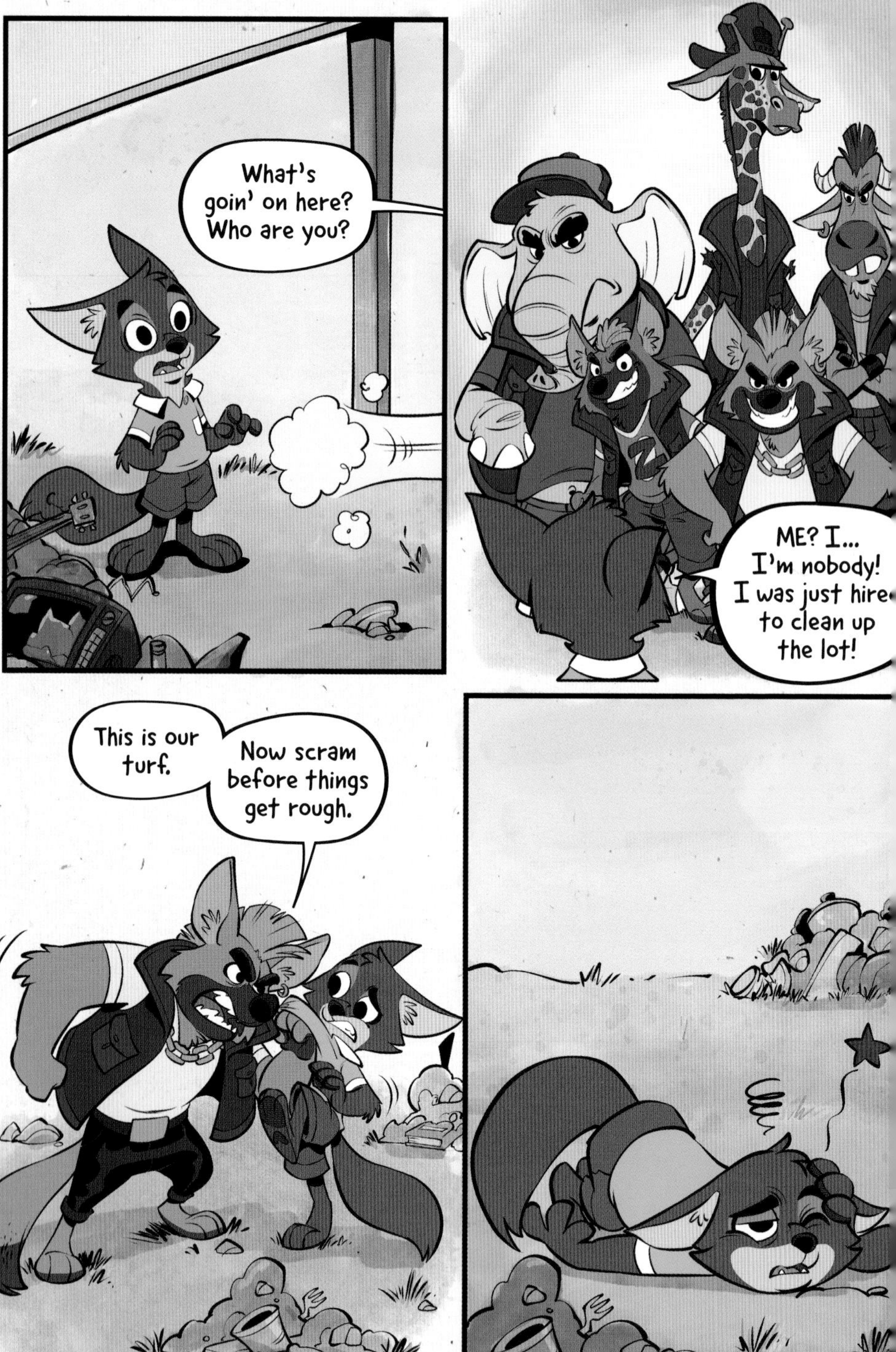
What's goin' on here? Who are you?
ME? I... I'm nobody! I was just hire to clean up the lot!
This is our turf.
Now scram before things get rough.

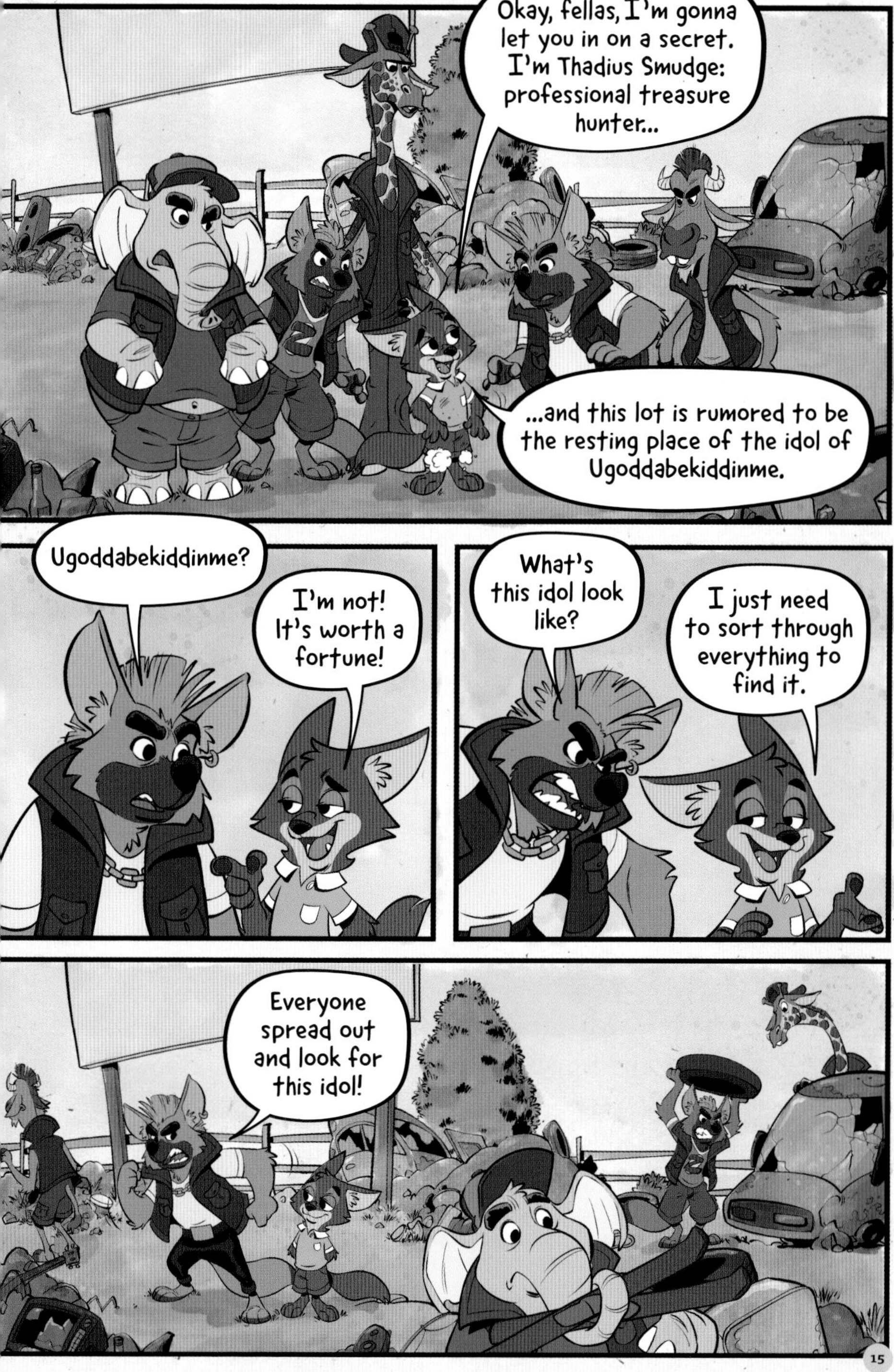
Okay, fellas, I'm gonna let you in on a secret. I'm Thadius Smudge: professional treasure hunter...
...and this lot is rumored to be the resting place of the idol of Ugoddabekiddinme.
Ugoddabekiddinme?
I'm not! It's worth a fortune!
What's this idol look like?
I just need to sort through everything to find it.
Everyone spread out and look for this idol!

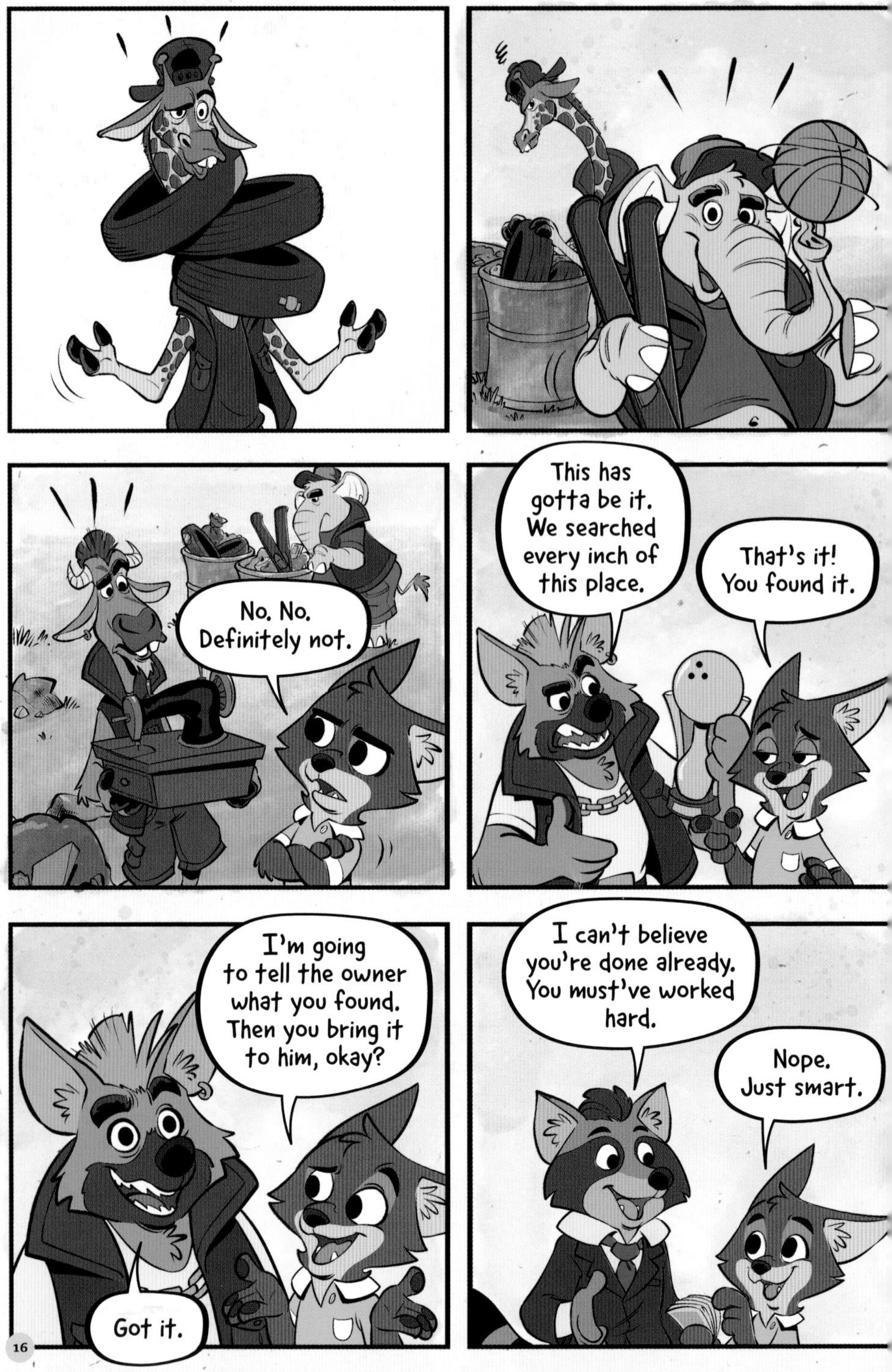
No. No.
Definitely not.
This has gotta be it. We searched every inch of this place.
That's it! You found it.
I'm going to tell the owner what you found. Then you bring it to him, okay?
Got it.
I can't believe you're done already. You must've worked hard.
Nope. Just smart.

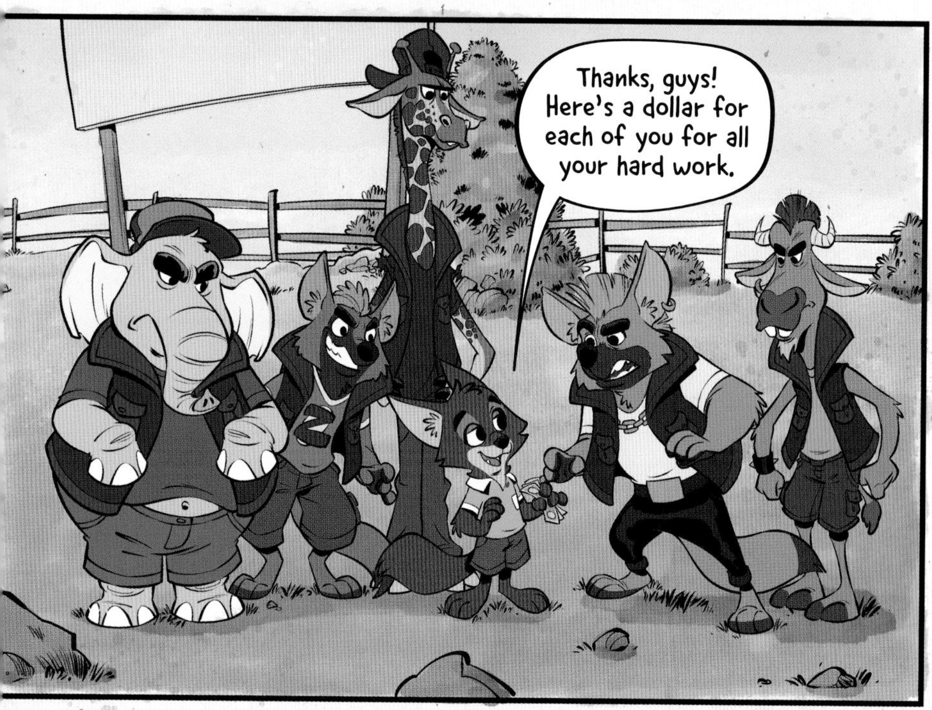
Thanks, guys! Here's a dollar for each of you for all your hard work.

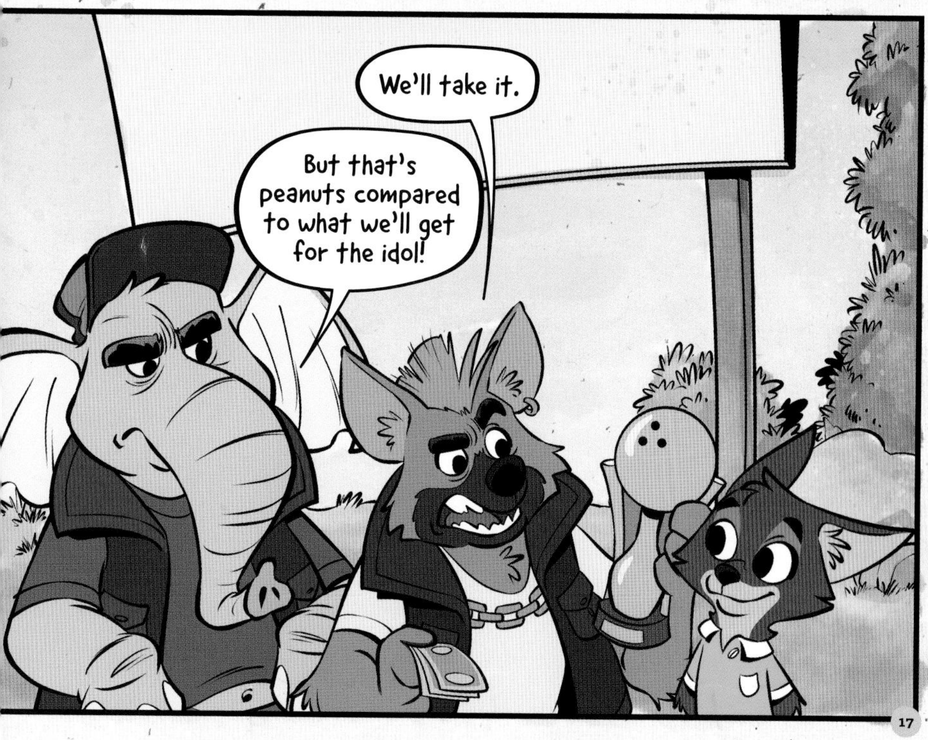
We'll take it.
But that's peanuts compared to what we'll get for the idol!

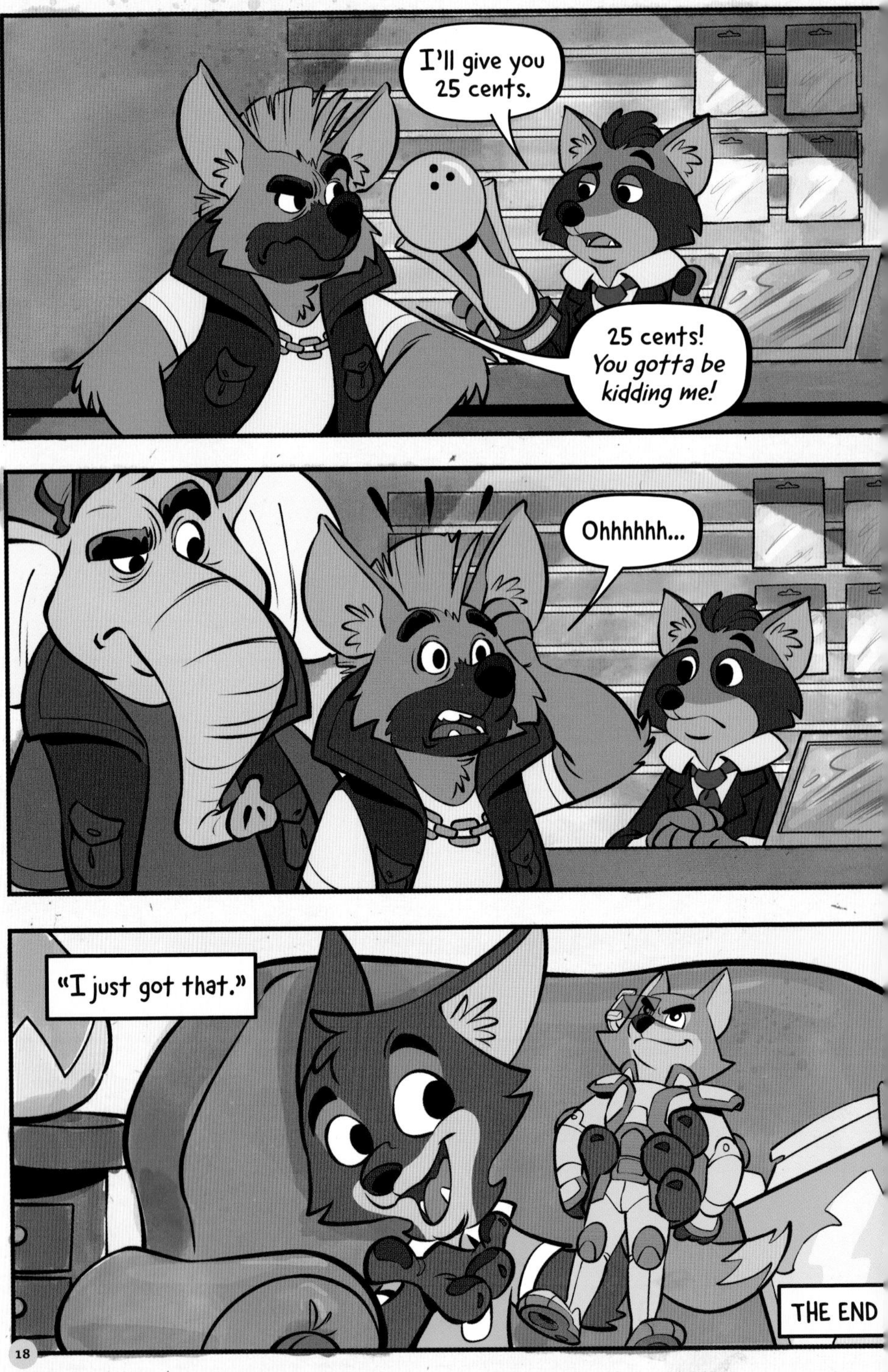
I'll give you 25 cents.
25 cents! You gotta be kidding me!
Ohhhhhh...
"I just got that."
THE END

Clueless

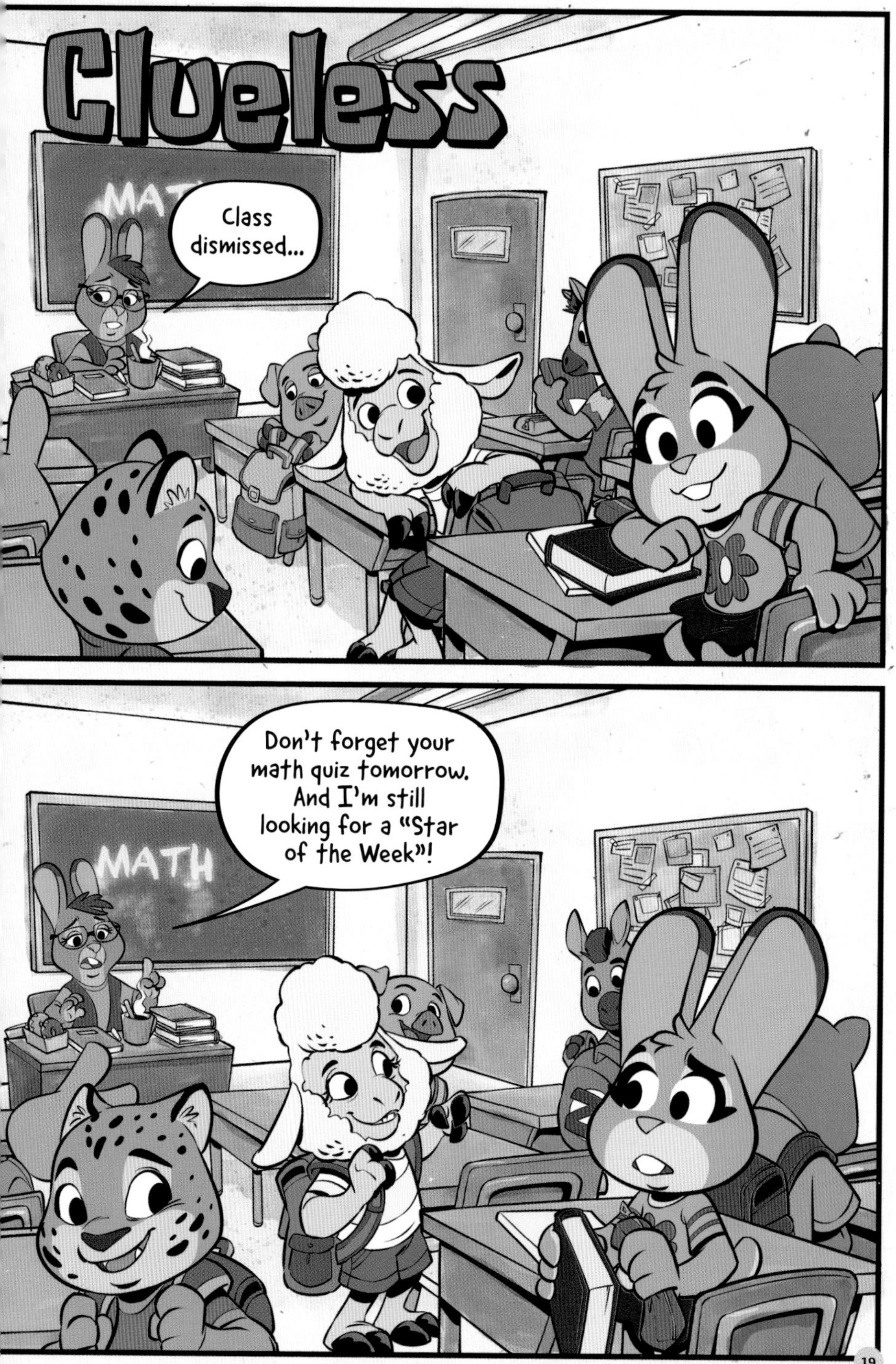
MATH
Class dismissed...
MATH
Don't forget your math quiz tomorrow. And I'm still looking for a "Star of the Week"!

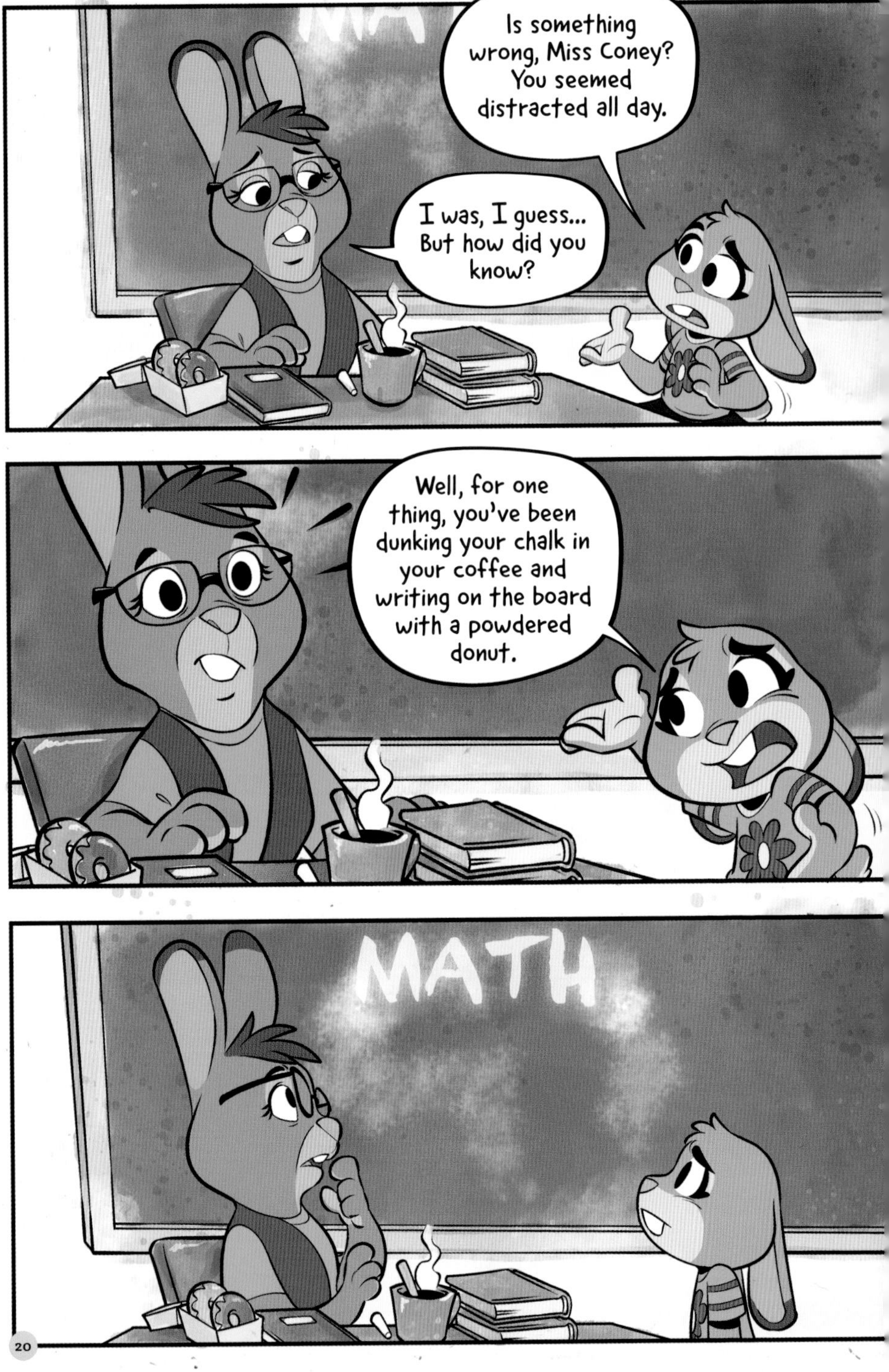

MA
Is something wrong, Miss Coney? You seemed distracted all day.
I was, I guess... But how did you know?
Well, for one thing, you've been dunking your chalk in your coffee and writing on the board with a powdered donut.
MATH

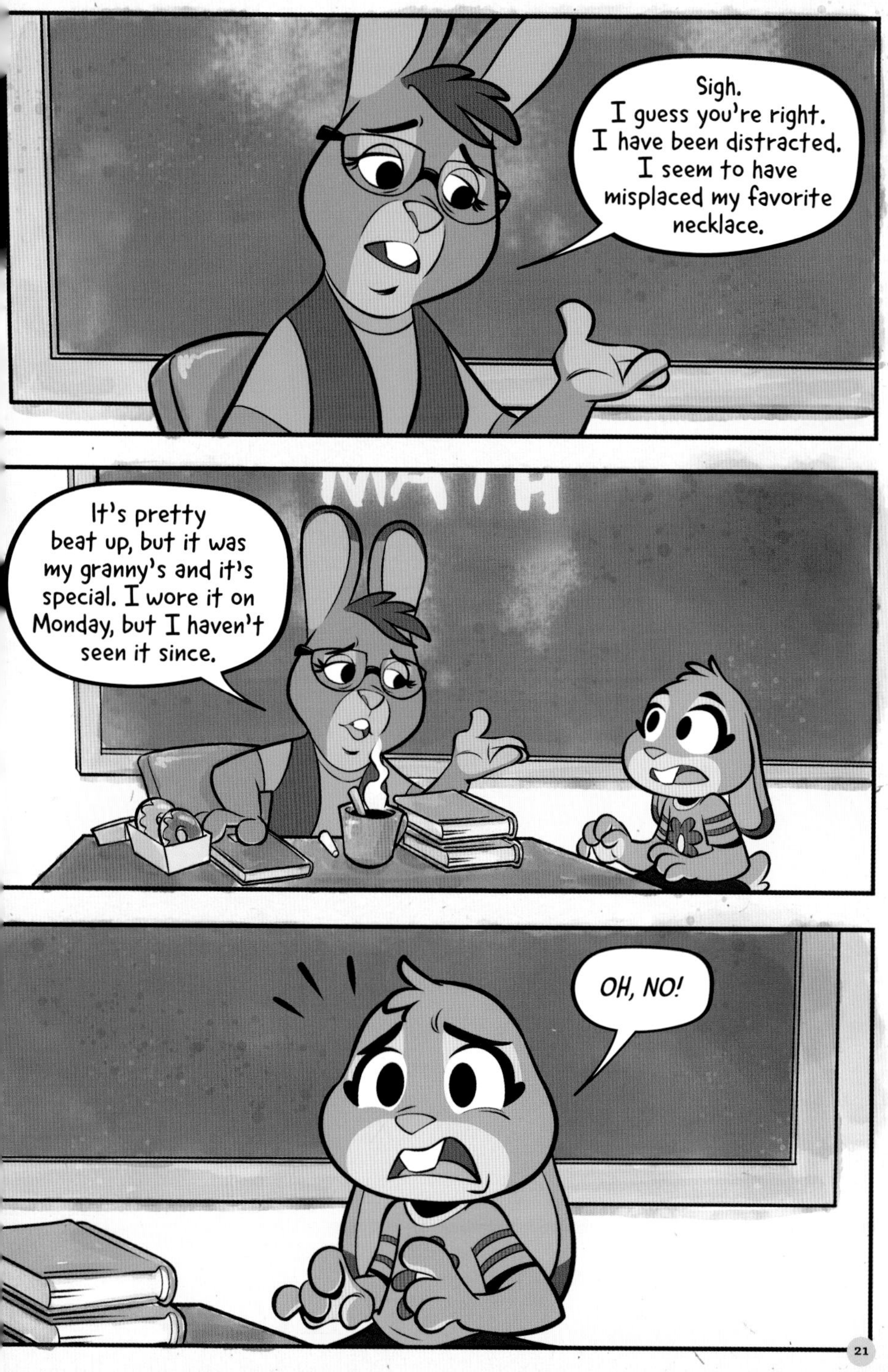
Sigh. I guess you're right. I have been distracted. I seem to have misplaced my favorite necklace.
MATH
It's pretty beat up, but it was my granny's and it's special. I wore it on Monday, but I haven't seen it since.
OH, NO!

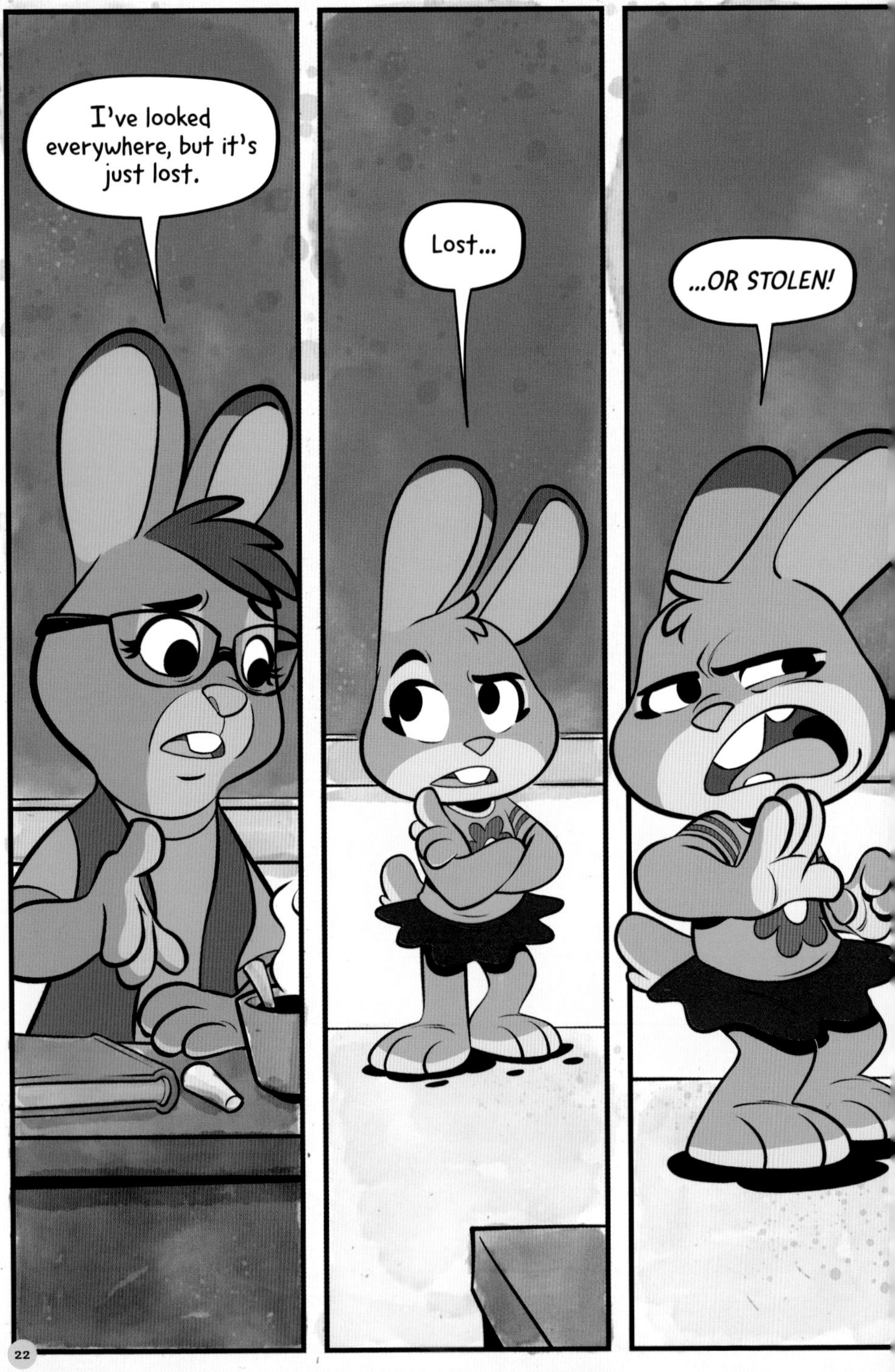
I've looked everywhere, but it's just lost.
Lost...
...OR STOLEN!

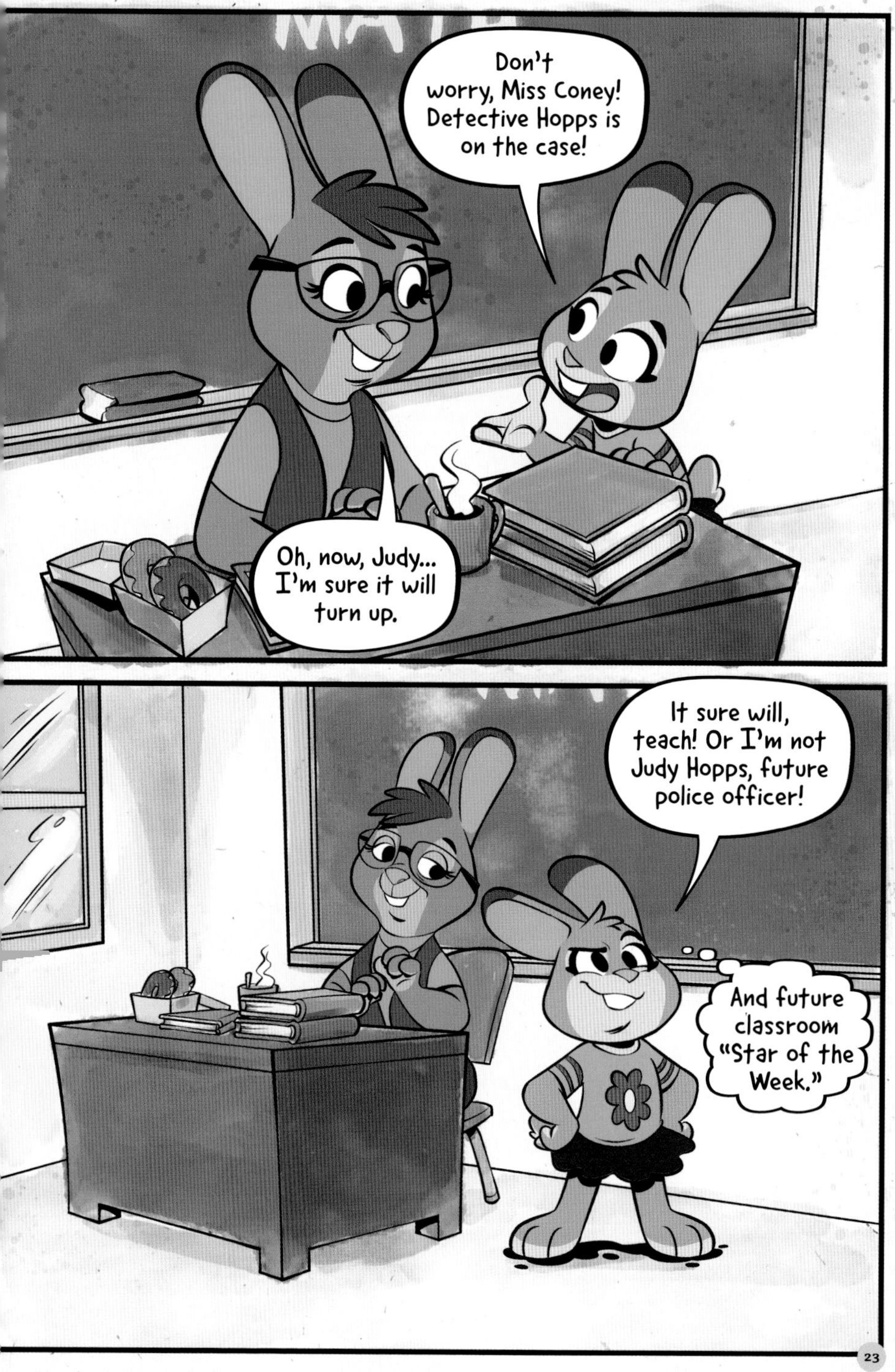
Don't worry, Miss Coney! Detective Hopps is on the case!
Oh, now, Judy... I'm sure it will turn up.
It sure will, teach! Or I'm not Judy Hopps, future police officer!
And future classroom "Star of the Week."

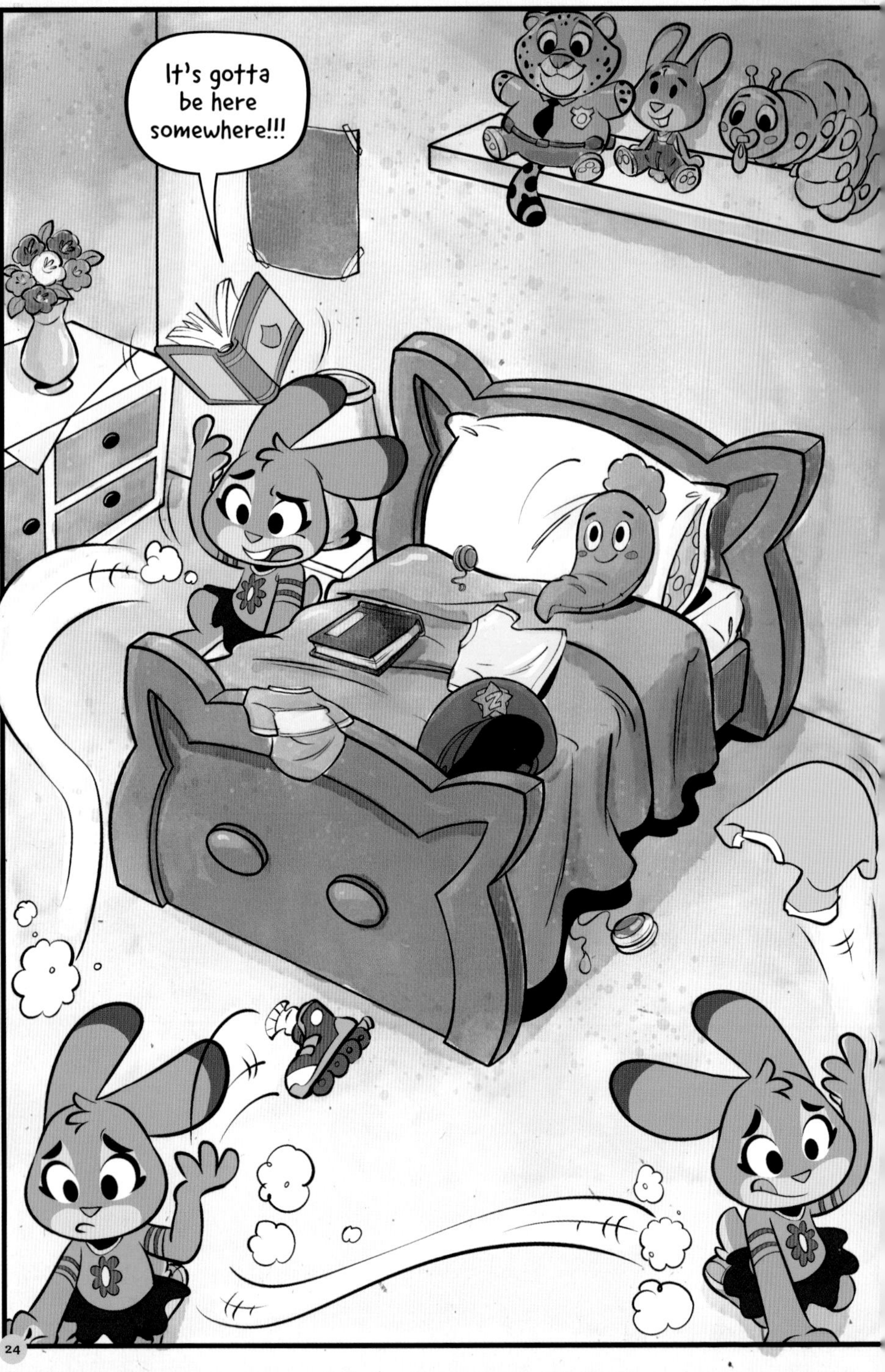
It's gotta be here somewhere!!!

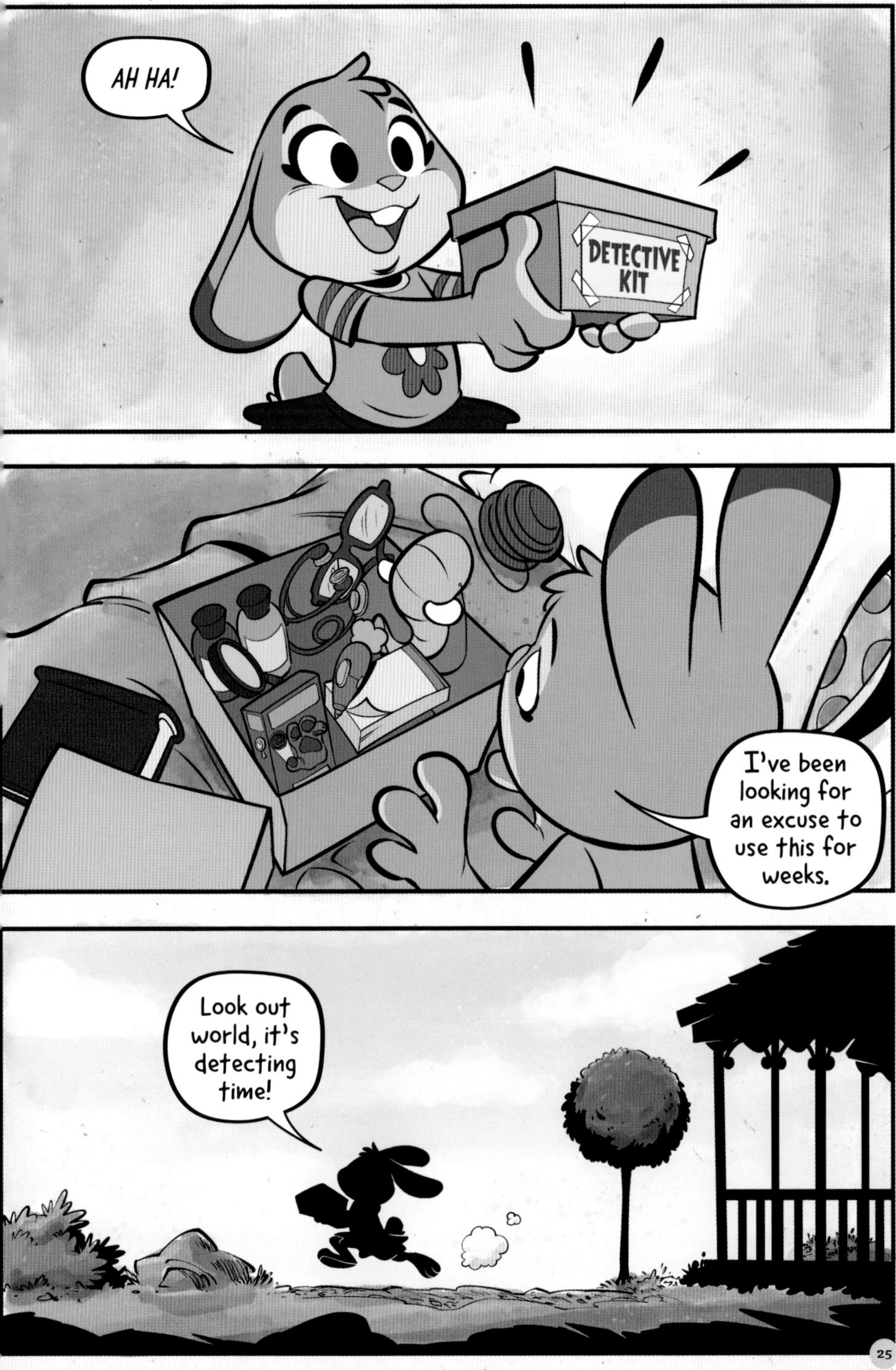
AH HA!
DETECTIVE KIT
I've been looking for an excuse to use this for weeks.
Look out world, it's detecting time!

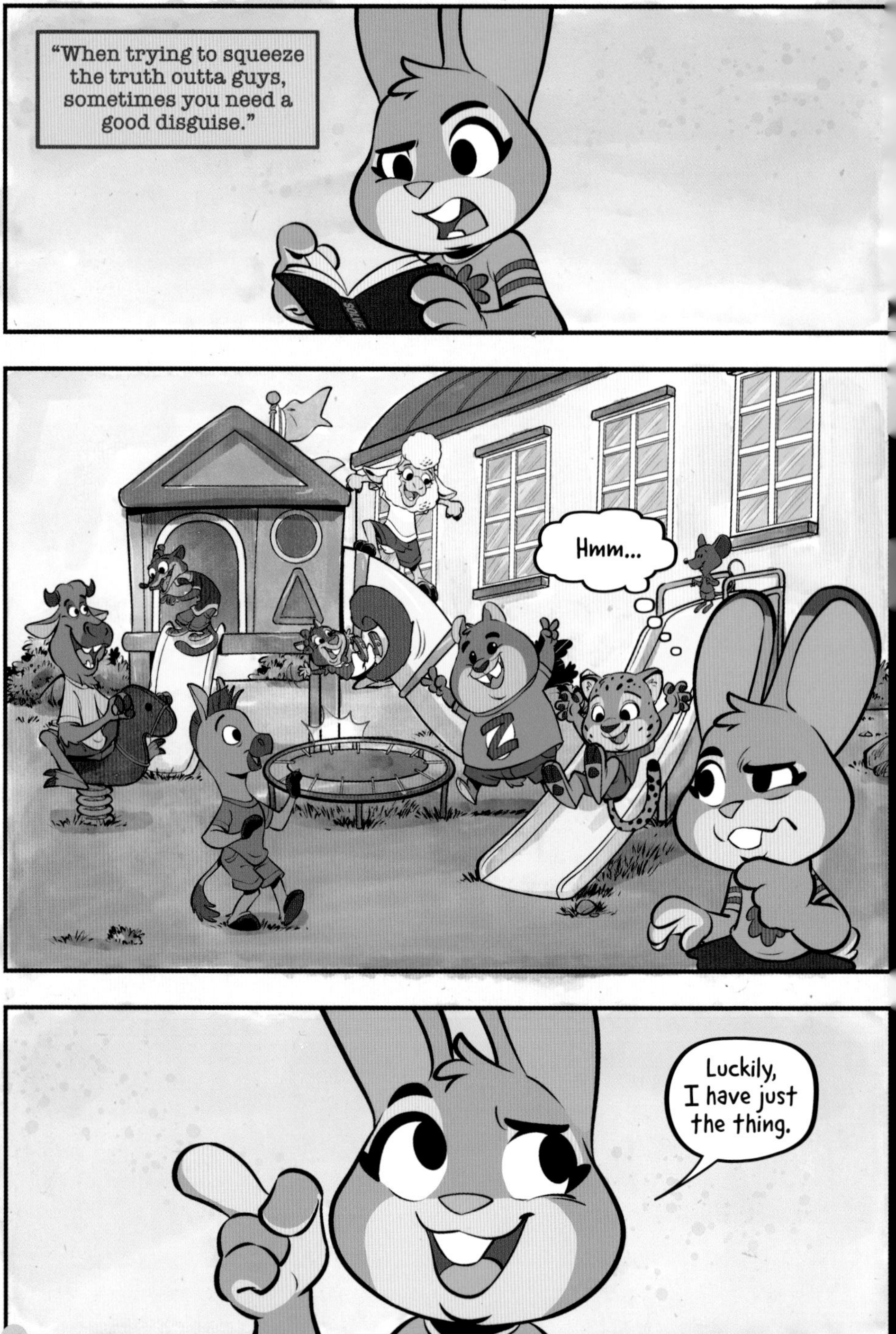
"When trying to squeeze the truth outta guys, sometimes you need a good disguise."
Hmm...
Luckily, I have just the thing.

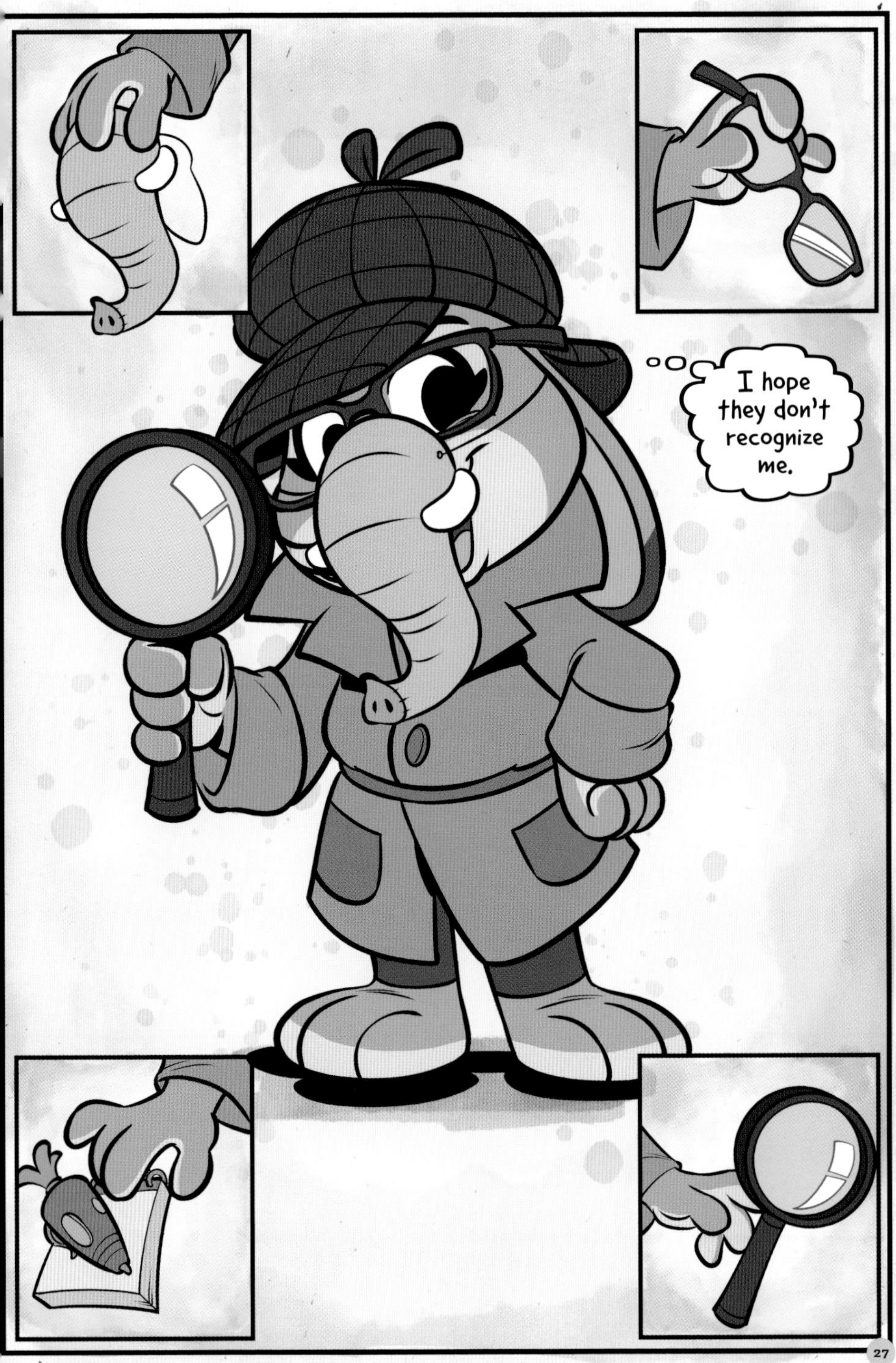
I hope they don't recognize me.

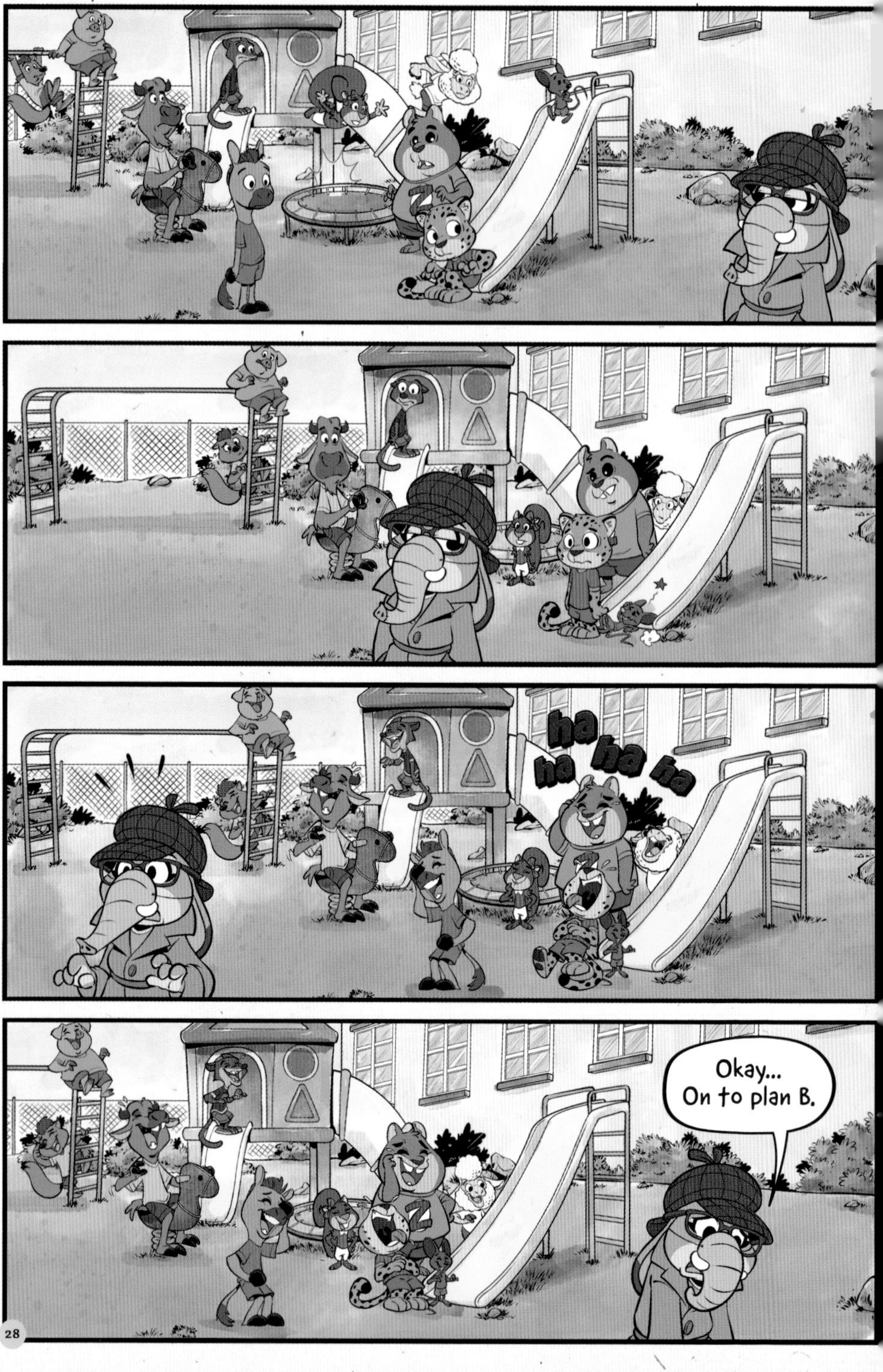
ha
ha ha ha
Okay...
On to plan B.

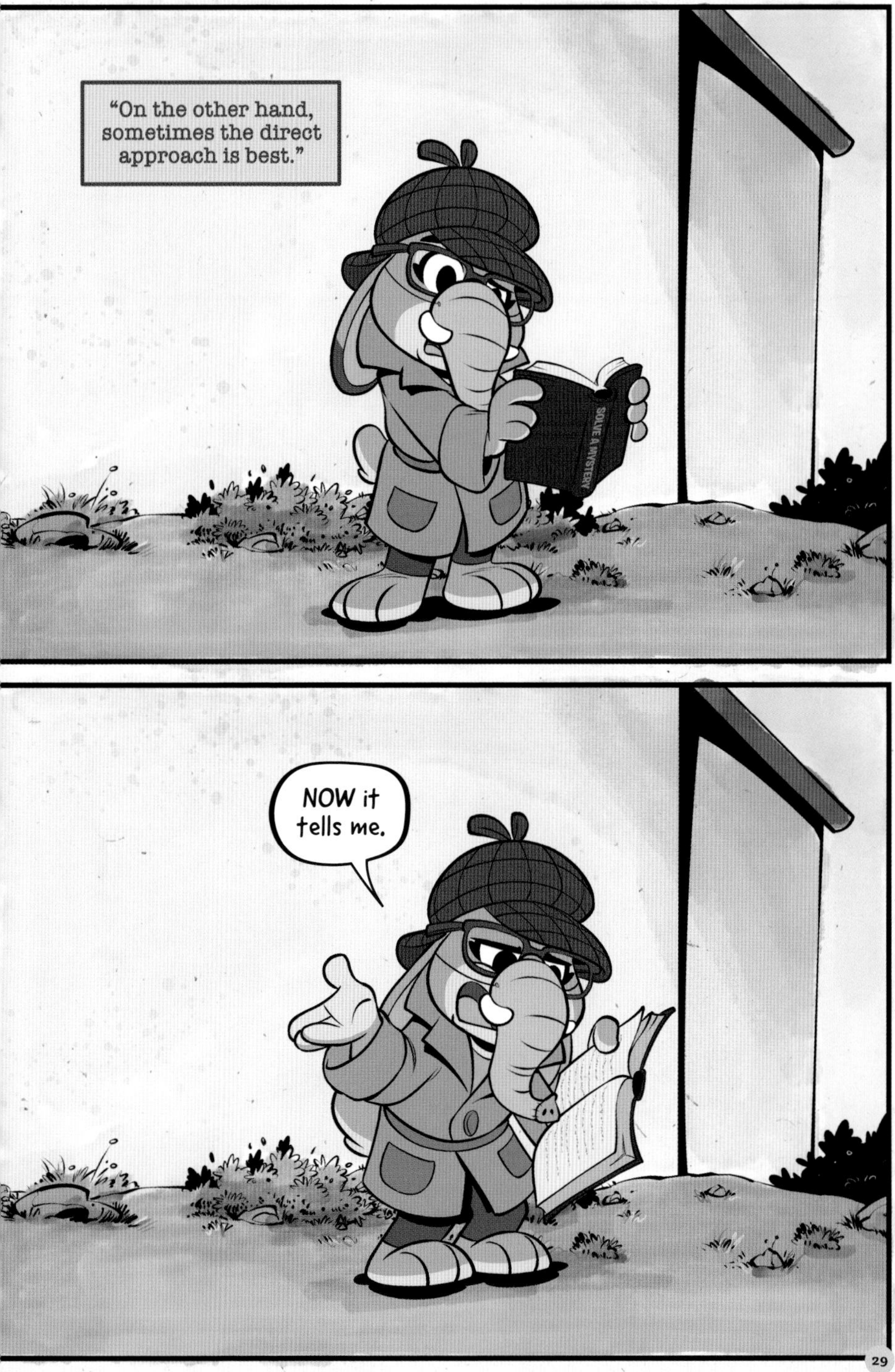
"On the other hand, sometimes the direct approach is best."
SOLVE A MYSTERY
NOW it tells me.

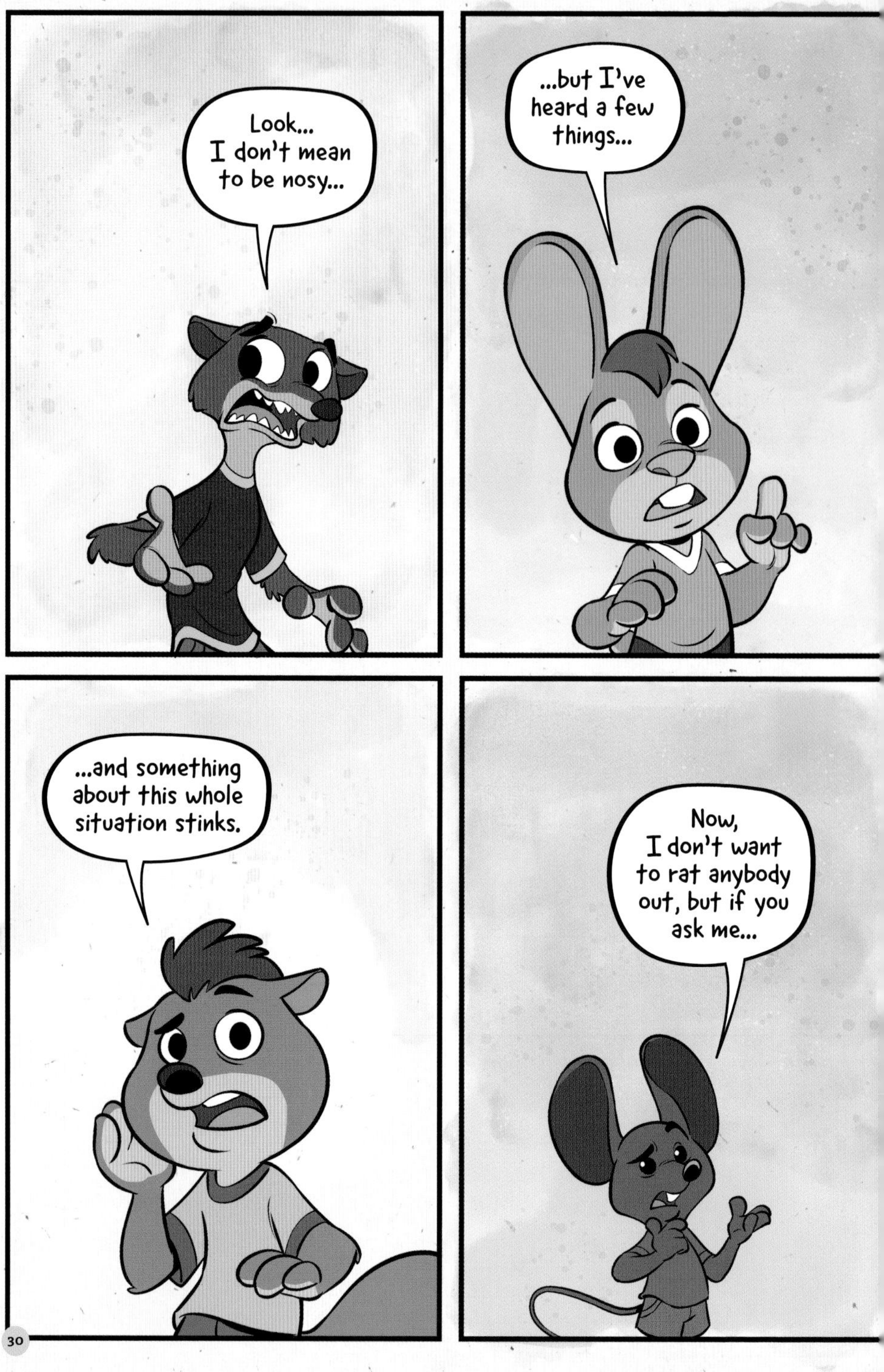
Look... I don't mean to be nosy...
...but I've heard a few things...
...and something about this whole situation stinks.
Now, I don't want to rat anybody out, but if you ask me...

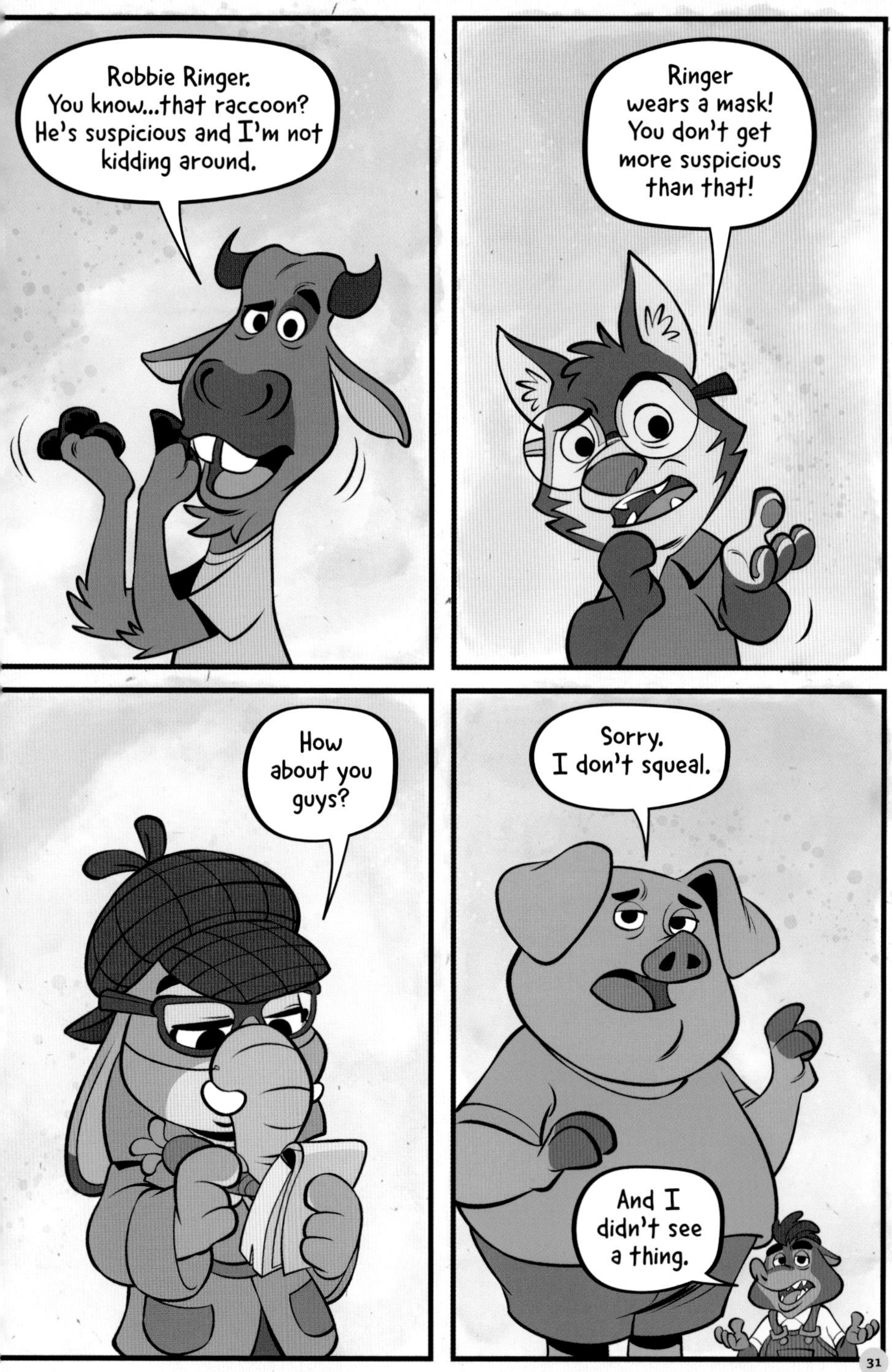
Robbie Ringer. You know...that raccoon? He's suspicious and I'm not kidding around.
Ringer wears a mask! You don't get more suspicious than that!
How about you guys?
Sorry. I don't squeal.
And I didn't see a thing.

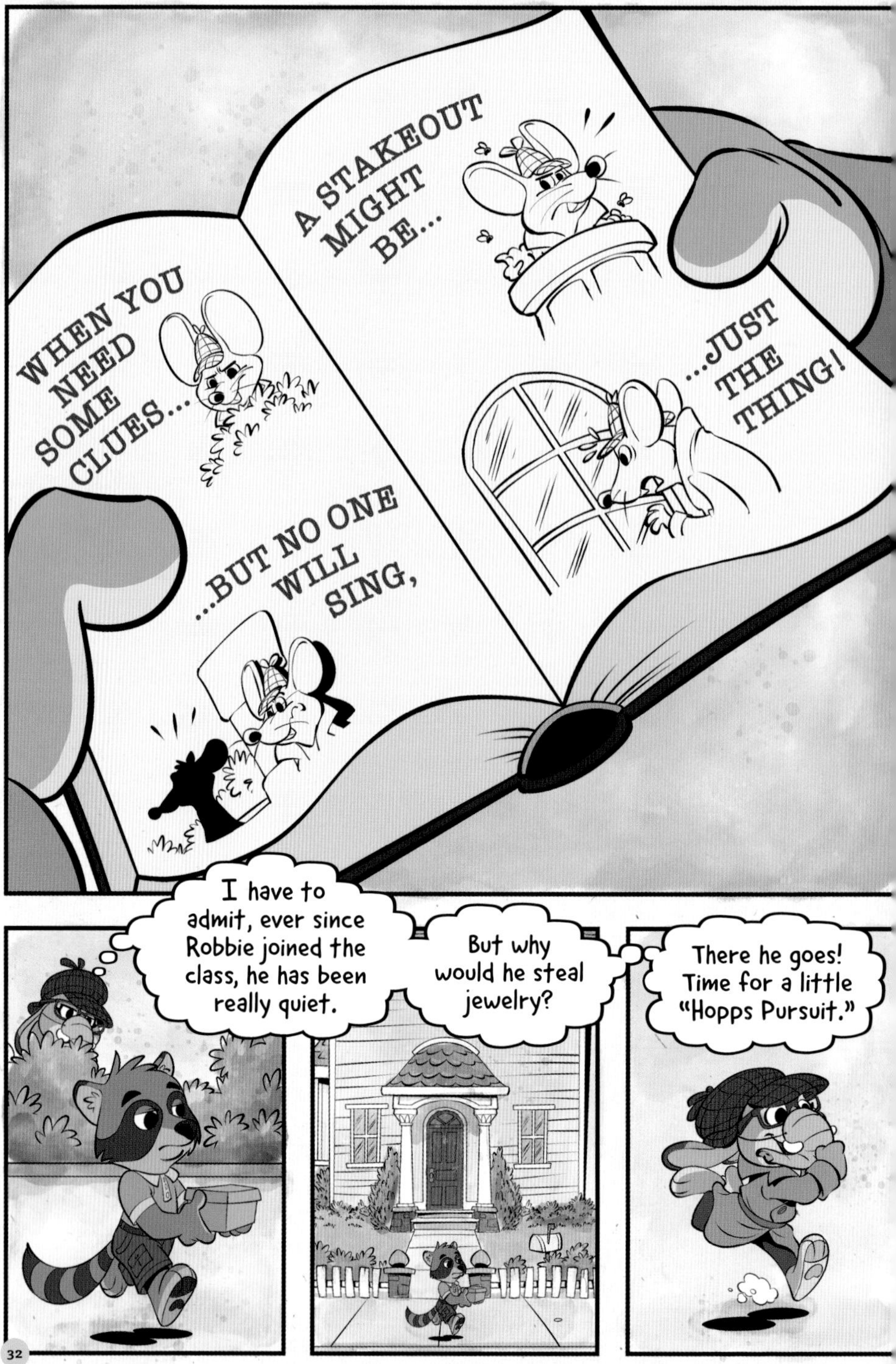
WHEN YOU NEED SOME CLUES...
...BUT NO ONE WILL SING,
A STAKEOUT MIGHT BE...
...JUST THE THING!
I have to admit, ever since Robbie joined the class, he has been really quiet.
But why would he steal jewelry?
There he goes! Time for a little "Hopps Pursuit."

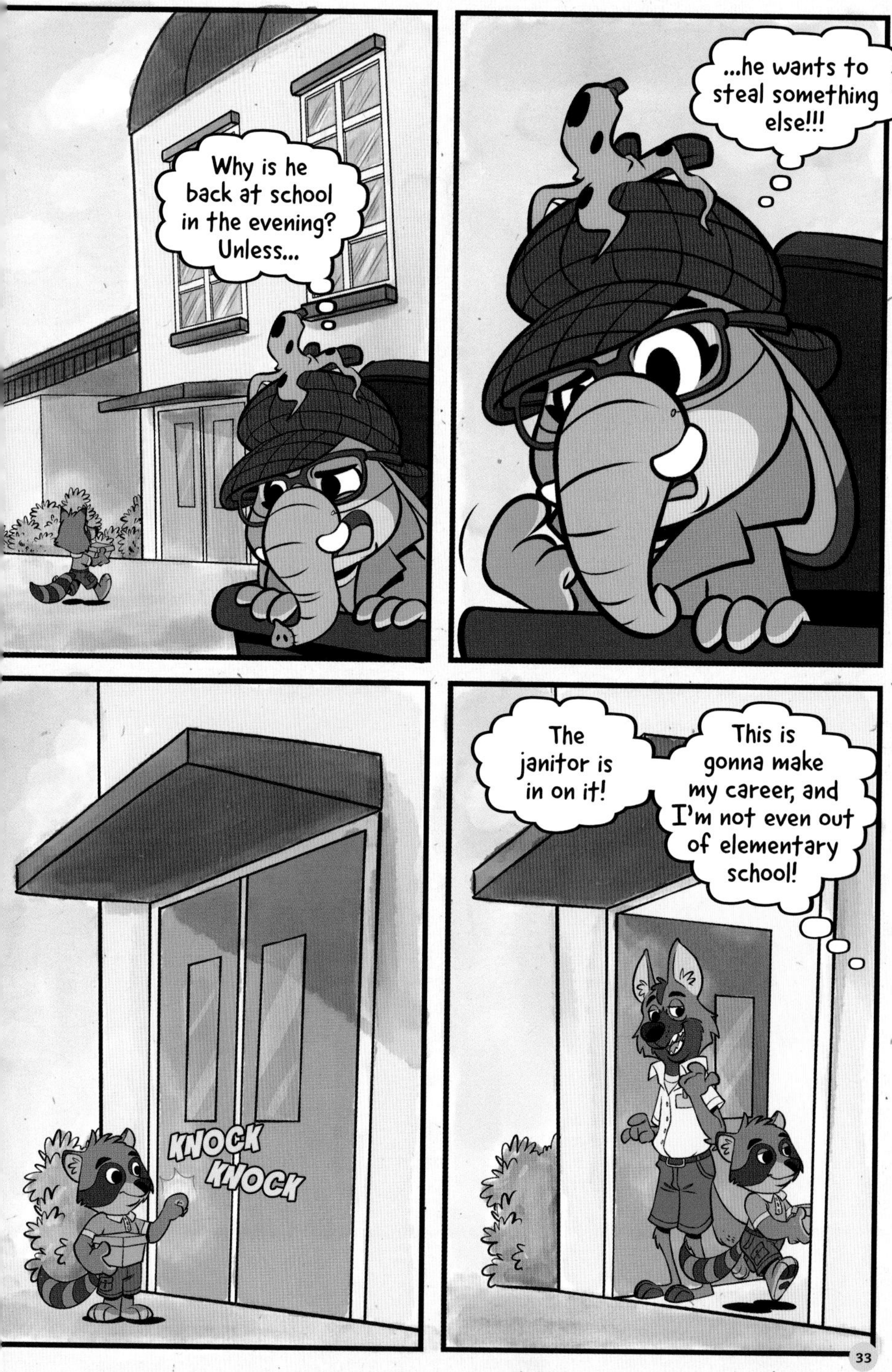
Why is he back at school in the evening? Unless...
...he wants to steal something else!!!
KNOCK KNOCK
The janitor is in on it!
This is gonna make my career, and I'm not even out of elementary school!

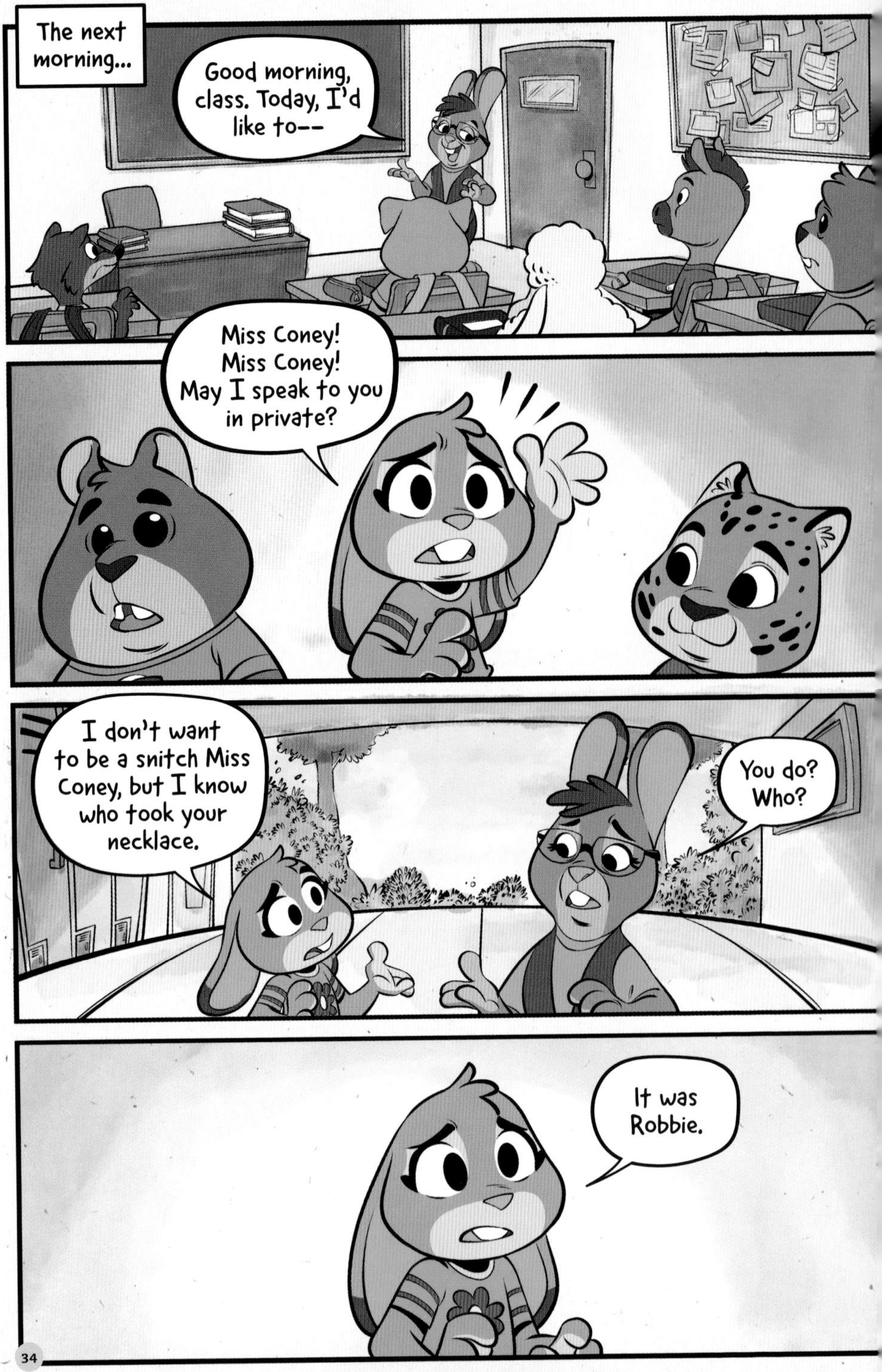
The next morning...
Good morning, class. Today, I'd like to--
Miss Coney! Miss Coney! May I speak to you in private?
I don't want to be a snitch Miss Coney, but I know who took your necklace.
You do? Who?
It was Robbie.

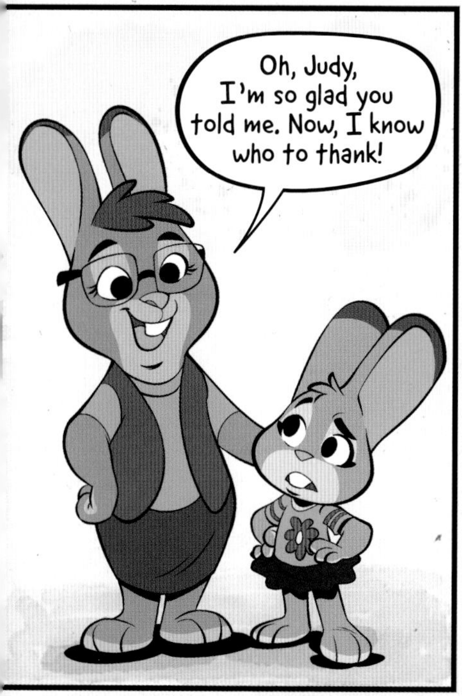
Oh, Judy, I'm so glad you told me. Now, I know who to thank!

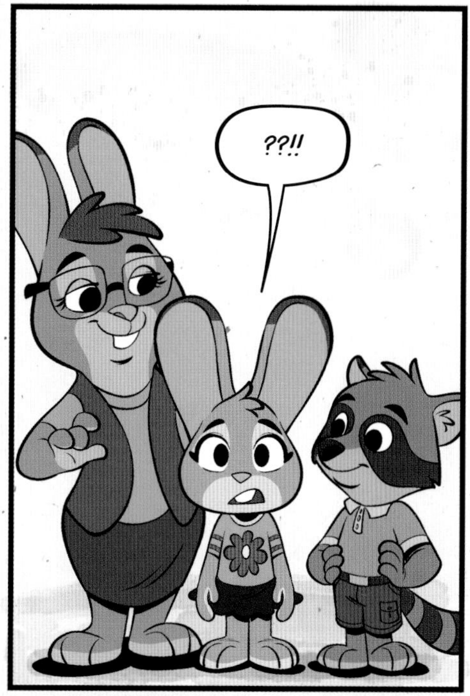
??!!

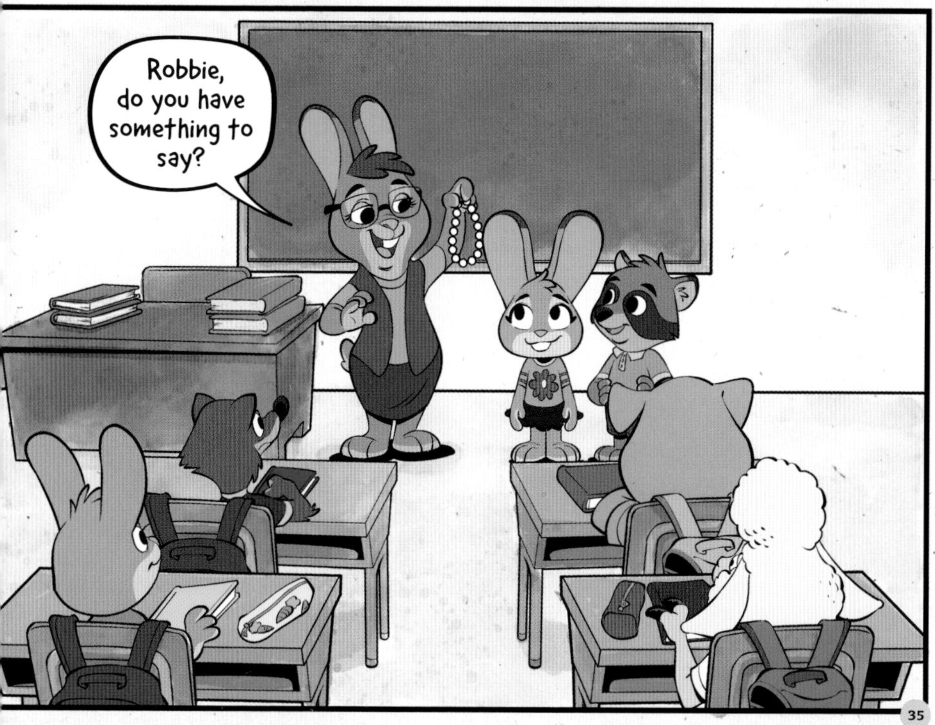
Robbie, do you have something to say?

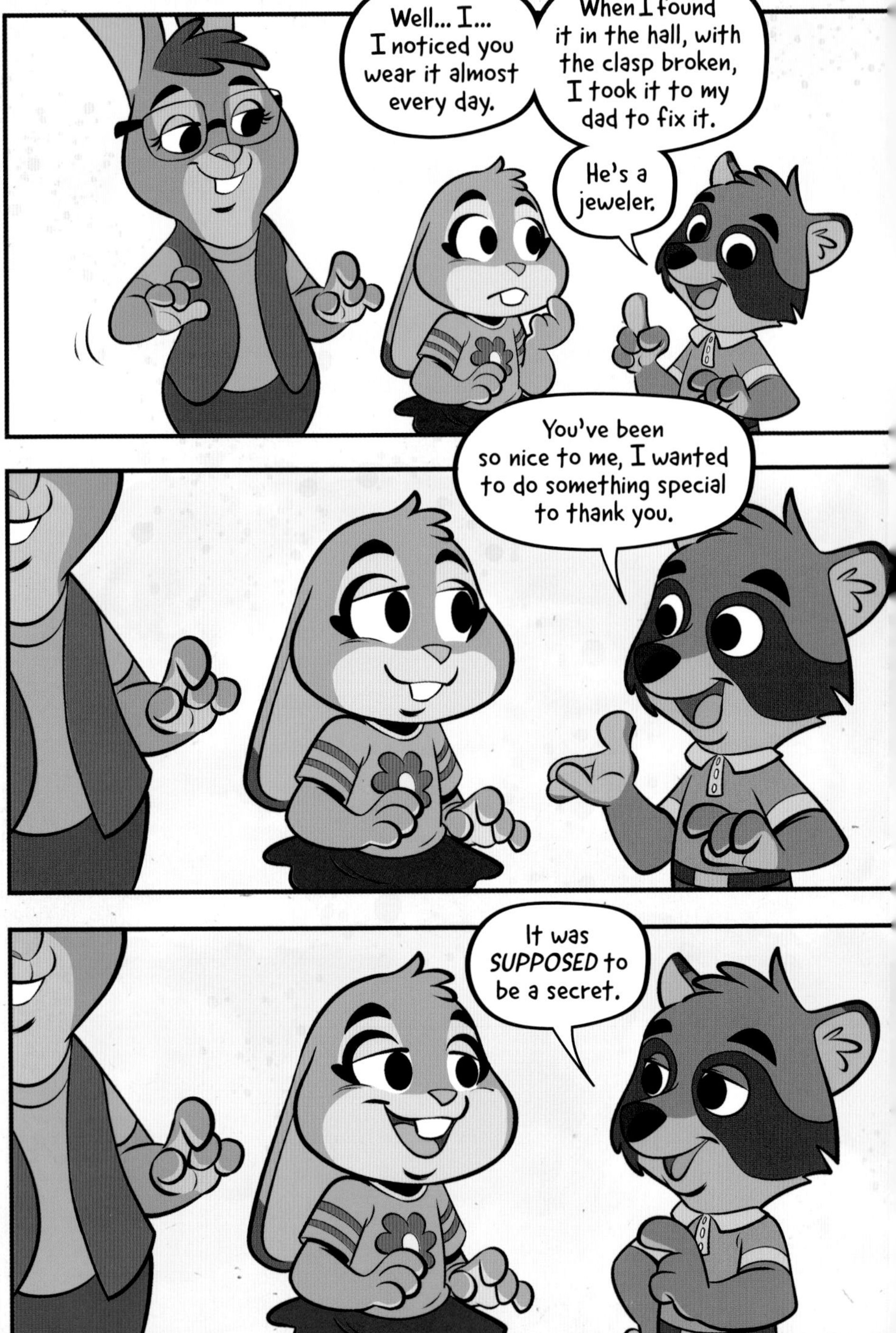
Well... I... I noticed you wear it almost every day.
When I found it in the hall, with the clasp broken, I took it to my dad to fix it.
He's a jeweler.
You've been so nice to me, I wanted to do something special to thank you.
It was *SUPPOSED* to be a secret.

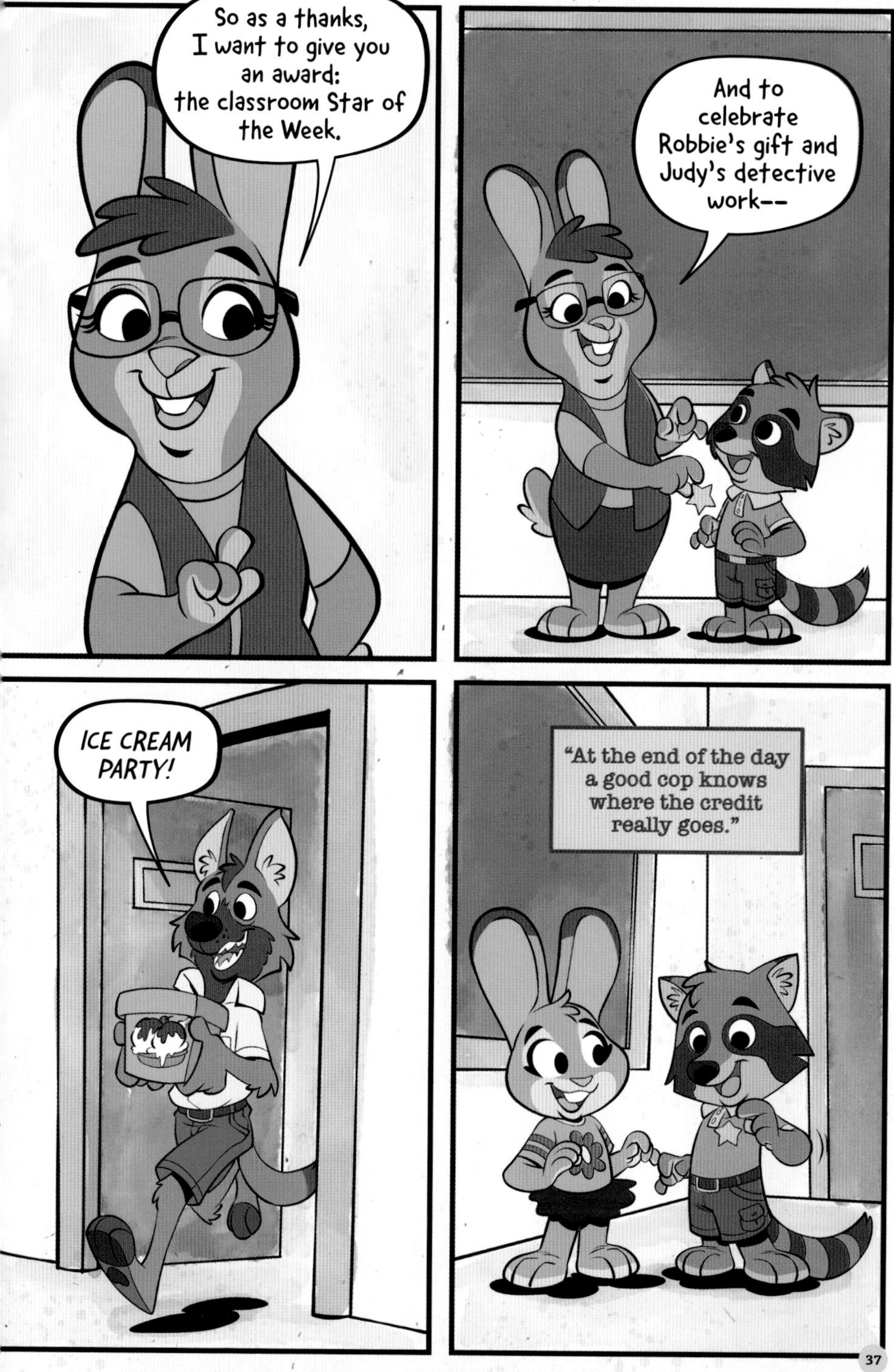
So as a thanks, I want to give you an award: the classroom Star of the Week.
And to celebrate Robbie's gift and Judy's detective work--
ICE CREAM PARTY!
"At the end of the day a good cop knows where the credit really goes."

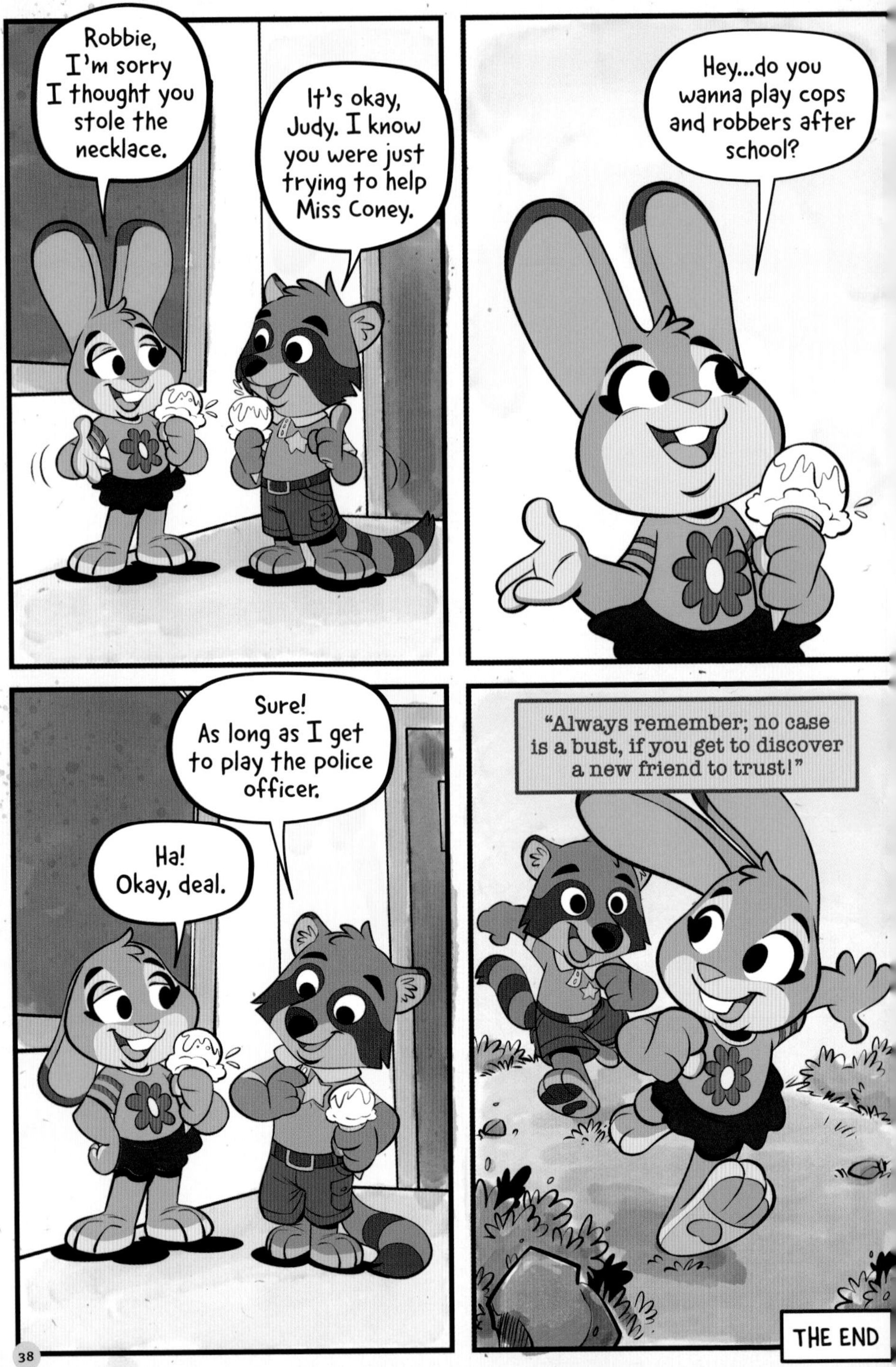
Robbie, I'm sorry I thought you stole the necklace.
It's okay, Judy. I know you were just trying to help Miss Coney.
Hey...do you wanna play cops and robbers after school?
Sure! As long as I get to play the police officer.
Ha! Okay, deal.
"Always remember; no case is a bust, if you get to discover a new friend to trust!"
THE END

WILD ACTIVITIES FOR EXTRA FUN!

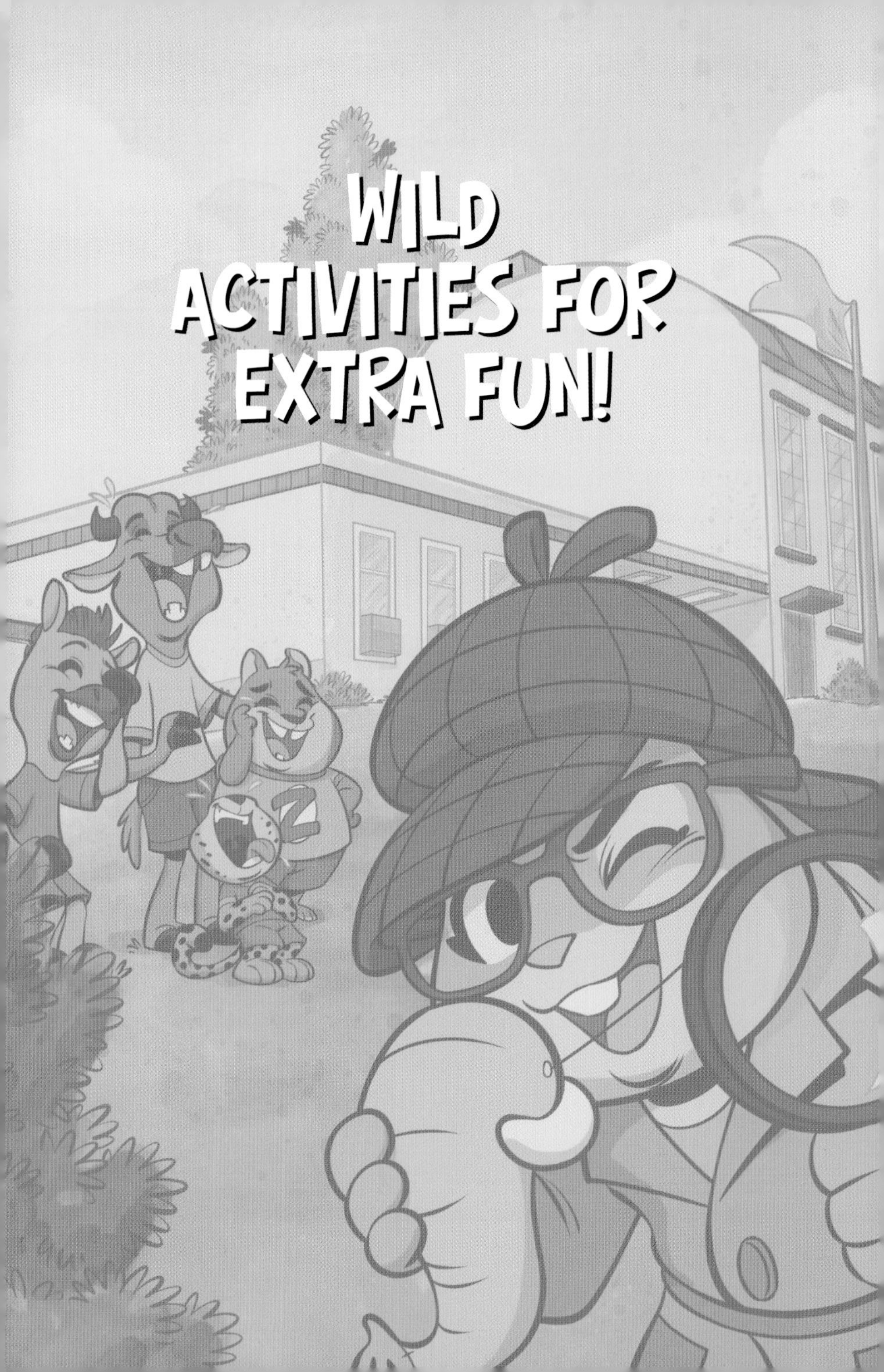

WHAT'S MISSING FROM THE PICTURE?

LOOK AT THE TWO PICTURES ON THESE PAGES OF NICK AND THE POSSE HE MEETS AT THE LOT. IT'S THE SAME PICTURE . . . OR IS IT? CAN YOU SPOT 10 DIFFERENCES BETWEEN PICTURE A, AND PICTURE B? THERE ARE SOME THINGS MISSING!

WHEN YOU THINK YOU'VE FOUND ALL THE DIFFERENCES YOU CAN CHECK YOUR ANSWERS AT THE BOTTOM OF PAGE 43!

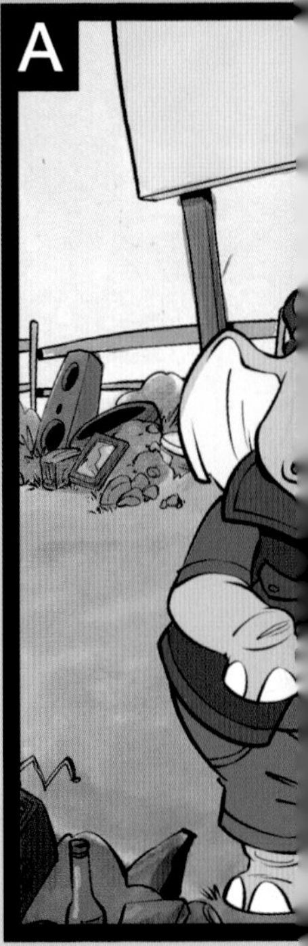
A

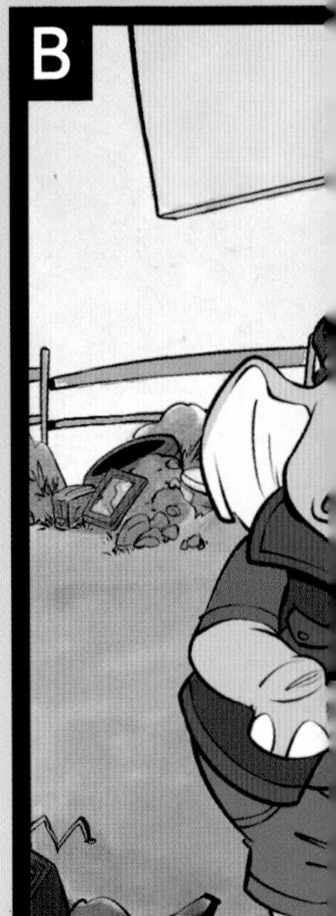
B

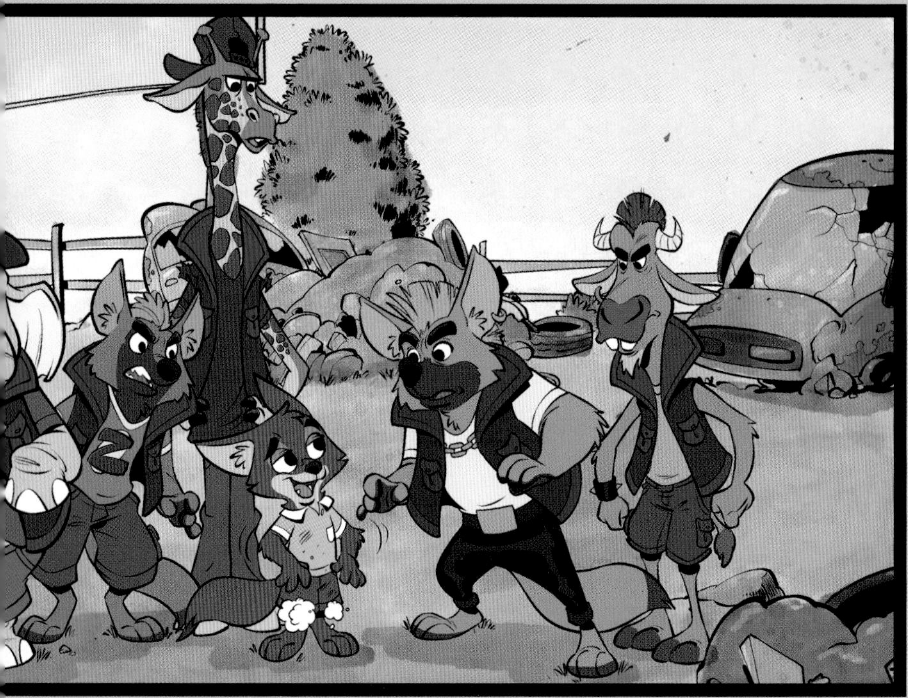

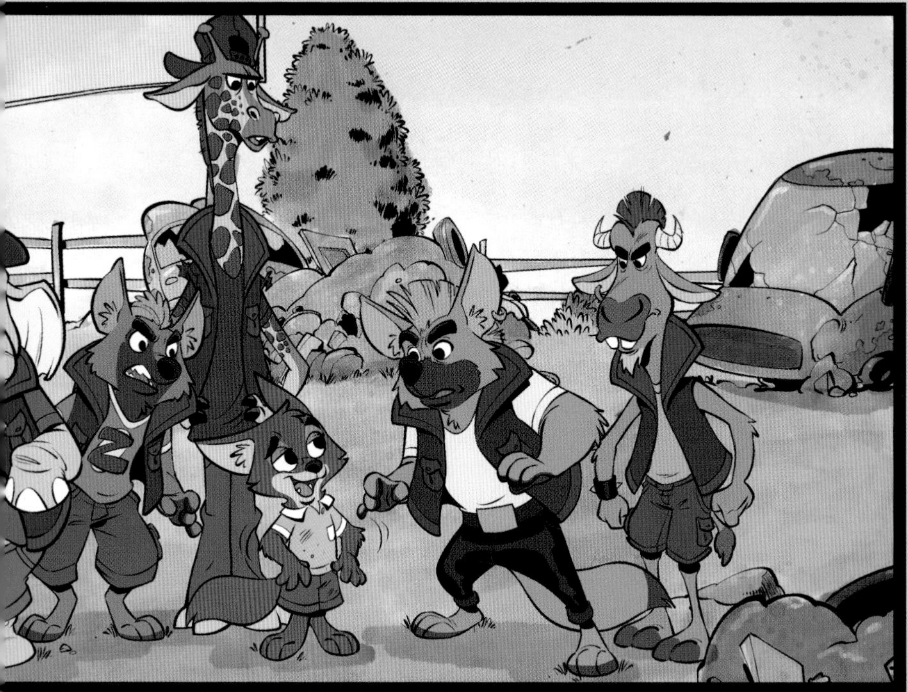

SCAVENGER HUNT!

CAN YOU FIND THESE ITEMS IN THE "AN ODD JOB" STORY?

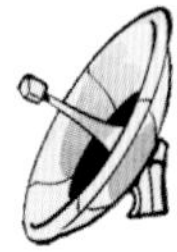

❶ **satellite dish**

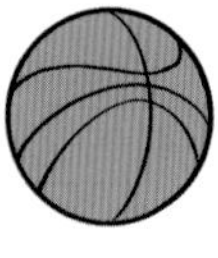

❷ **basketball**

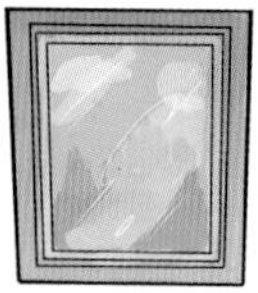

❸ **picture frame**

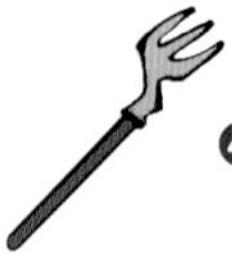

❹ **fork**

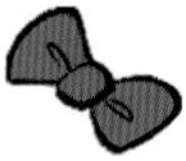

❺ **purple bow**

CAN YOU FIND THESE ITEMS IN THE "CLUELESS" STORY?

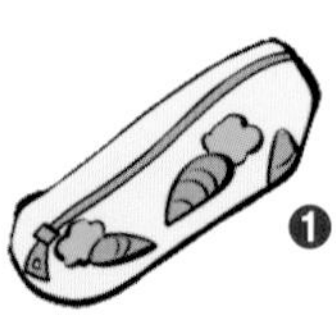

❶ **pencil case**

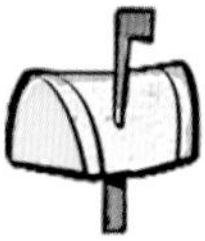

❷ **mailbox**

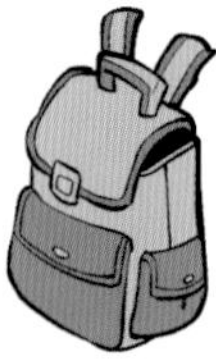

❸ **blue backpack**

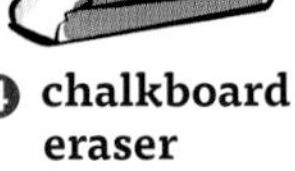

❹ **chalkboard eraser**

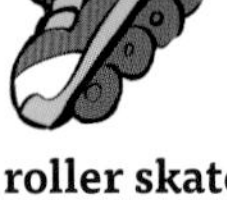

❺ **roller skate**

Scavenger Hunt answer key:
"An Odd Job": satellite dish, page 13; basketball, page 16; picture frame, page 7; fork, page 14; purple bow, page 11

Scavenger Hunt answer key:
"Clueless": pencil case, page 35; mailbox, page 32; blue backpack, page 19; chalkboard eraser, page 23; roller skate, page 24

WHAT HAPPENS NEXT?

THE QUEST TO FIND MISS CONEY'S NECKLACE PROVED TO BE A SUCCESS FOR JUDY—GETTING TO USE HER SUPERB DETECTIVE SKILLS AND BEST OF ALL—MEETING A NEW FRIEND TO SHARE IN HER CURIOSITIES AND ADVENTURES!

Now that Judy has solved one mystery, can you think about what other mysteries are on the horizon that Judy and Robbie could team up to solve?

Write a story or draw a picture of what happens next! Use any of the characters in the story. Take another walk through the playground and see what you can come up with!

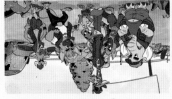

What's Missing from the Picture answer key:

WHAT'S MISSING F

LOOK AT THE TWO PICTURES ON THESE PAGES OF JUDY IN CLASS. IT'S THE SAME PICTURE . . . OR IS IT? CAN YOU SPOT 10 DIFFERENCES BETWEEN PICTURE A, AND PICTURE B? THERE ARE SOME THINGS MISSING!

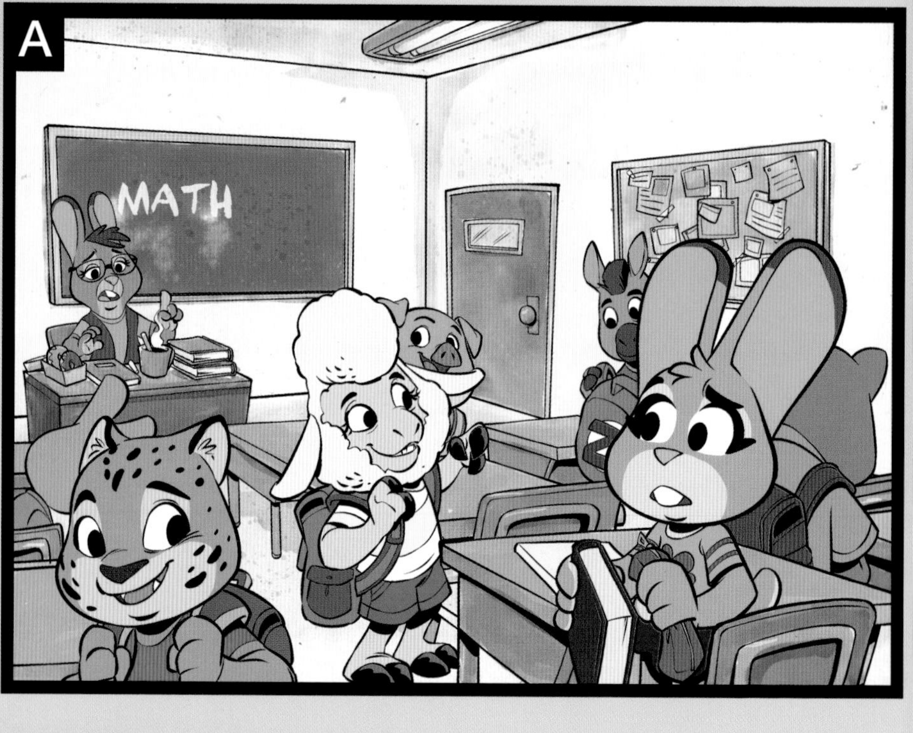
A
MATH

OM THE PICTURE?

WHEN YOU THINK YOU'VE FOUND ALL THE DIFFERENCES, YOU CAN CHECK YOUR ANSWERS AT THE BOTTOM OF PAGE 46!

B

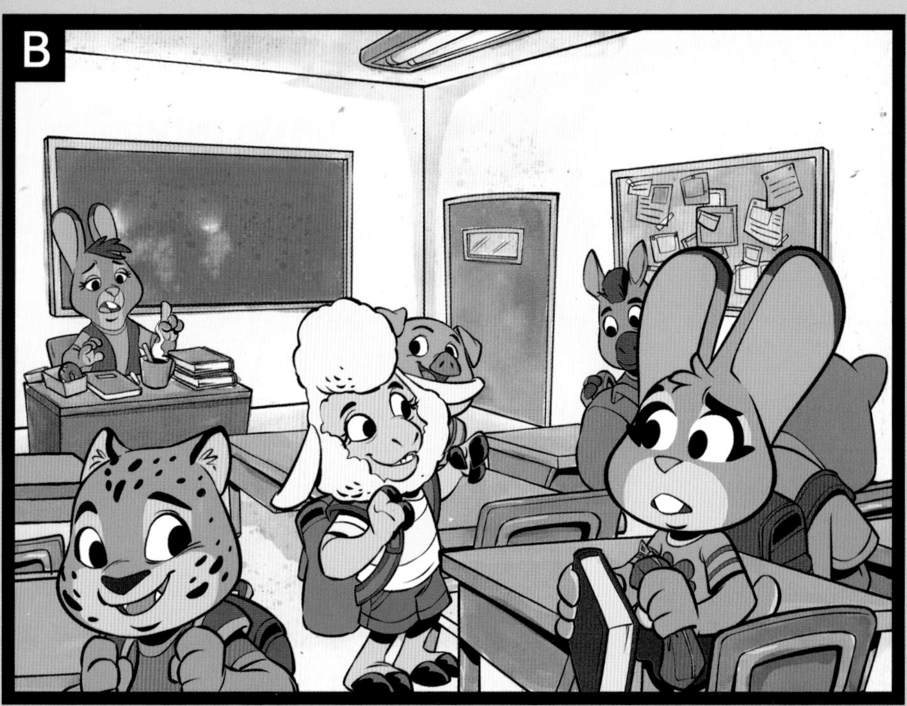

RHYME TIME!

LET'S PLAY A FUN GAME OF RHYMING! FOR THIS GAME, YOU CAN PLAY WITH A PARTNER OR BY YOURSELF! REMEMBER TO GIVE YOURSELF SOME SPACE TO PLAY! YOU WILL NEED:

-SOME PIECES OF SCRAP PAPER OR INDEX CARDS

-ONE CONTAINER (a bowl or box)

1 Let's return to Nick's story "An Odd Job"!
On each of the pieces of paper (or index cards), write down a single syllable word from the story.

Some of these words are:
Nick, Fox, Toy, Job, Cents

Try to write down at least five words. Lay each of these pieces of paper on the floor or table, spread out in front of you.

2 Looking at each of these words you laid out, think of some words that rhyme with them. Write each of the rhyming words down on pieces of paper, or cards.

Some examples of rhyming words for "Fox" are:
Box, Socks, Shocks, Blocks, etc.

Once you have at least five rhyming words written down for each of the original words, put these scraps of paper into the bowl or box and mix them up!

3 Next, pull out a word, one by one, from the container. Try to match each word with the original word that it rhymes with. Simply place that word next to the original word you laid out. Do this until your container of rhyming words is empty!

*For an added challenge, use a timer and try to sort all the words as fast as you can.

What's Missing from the Picture answer key:

DARK HORSE BOOKS

president and publisher Mike Richardson • collection editor Freddye Miller •
collection assistant editor Judy Khuu • collection designer David Nestelle •
digital art technician Christianne Gillenardo-Goudreau

Neil Hankerson Executive Vice President • Tom Weddle Chief Financial Officer • Randy Stradley Vice President of Publishing • Nick McWhorter Chief Business Development Officer • Dale LaFountain Chief Information Officer • Matt Parkinson Vice President of Marketing • Cara Niece Vice President of Production and Scheduling • Mark Bernardi Vice President of Book Trade and Digital Sales • Ken Lizzi General Counsel • Dave Marshall Editor in Chief • Davey Estrada Editorial Director • Chris Warner Senior Books Editor • Cary Grazzini Director of Specialty Projects • Lia Ribacchi Art Director • Vanessa Todd-Holmes Director of Print Purchasing • Matt Dryer Director of Digital Art and Prepress • Michael Gombos Senior Director of Licensed Publications • Kari Yadro Director of Custom Programs • Kari Torson Director of International Licensing • Sean Brice Director of Trade Sales

DISNEY PUBLISHING WORLDWIDE GLOBAL MAGAZINES, COMICS AND PARTWORKS

PUBLISHER Lynn Waggoner • EDITORIAL TEAM Bianca Coletti (Director, Magazines), Guido Frazzini (Director, Comics), Carlotta Quattrocolo (Executive Editor), Stefano Ambrosio (Executive Editor, New IP), Camilla Vedove (Senior Manager, Editorial Development), Behnoosh Khalili (Senior Editor), Julie Dorris (Senior Editor), Mina Riazi (Assistant Editor), Jonathan Manning (Assistant Editor) • DESIGN Enrico Soave (Senior Designer) • ART Ken Shue (VP, Global Art), Manny Mederos (Senior Illustration Manager, Comics and Magazines), Roberto Santillo (Creative Director), Marco Ghiglione (Creative Manager), Stefano Attardi (Computer Art Designer) • PORTFOLIO MANAGEMENT Olivia Ciancarelli (Director) • BUSINESS & MARKETING Mariantonietta Galla (Marketing Manager), Virpi Korhonen (Editorial Manager)

Zootopia: A Hard Day's Work

Published by Dark Horse Books
A division of Dark Horse Comics LLC
10956 SE Main Street
Milwaukie, OR 97222

DarkHorse.com

To find a comics shop in your area, visit comicshoplocator.com

First edition: July 2019
ISBN 978-1-50671-206-2
Digital ISBN 978-1-50671-208-6

1 3 5 7 9 10 8 6 4 2
Printed in China

Disney PIXAR
INCREDIBLES 2
Heroes at Home
Disney COMICS

LOOKING FOR BOOKS FOR YOUNGER READERS?

$7.99 each!

EACH VOLUME INCLUDES A SECTION OF FUN ACTIVITIES!

A Graphic Novel for Younger Readers
Disney
ZOOTOPIA
FRIENDS TO THE RESCUE
COUNTY FAIR
Disney COMICS

A Graphic Novel for Younger Readers
Disney
ZOOTOPIA
FAMILY NIGHT
Disney COMICS

A Graphic Novel for Younger Readers
Disney
PRINCESS
Jasmine's New Pet
Disney COMICS

A Graphic Novel for Younger Readers
Disney
PRINCESS
Ariel and the Sea Wolf
Disney COMICS

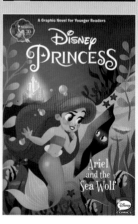

DISNEY ZOOTOPIA: FRIENDS TO THE RESCUE

ISBN 978-1-50671-054-9

DISNEY ZOOTOPIA: FAMILY NIGHT

ISBN 978-1-50671-053-2

Join young Judy Hopps as she uses wit and bravery to solve mysteries, conundrums, and more! And quick-thinking young Nick Wilde won't be stopped from achieving his goals—where there's a will, there's a way!

DISNEY•PIXAR INCREDIBLES 2: HEROES AT HOME

ISBN 978-1-50670-943-7

Being part of a Super family means helping out at home, too. Can Violet and Dash pick up groceries and secretly stop some bad guys? And can they clean up the house while Jack-Jack is "sleeping"?

DISNEY PRINCESS: JASMINE'S NEW PET

ISBN 978-1-50671-052-5

Jasmine has a new pet tiger, Rajah, but he's not quite ready for palace life. Will she be able to train the young cub before the Sultan finds him another home?

DISNEY PRINCESS: ARIEL AND THE SEA WOLF

ISBN 978-1-50671-203-1

Ariel accidentally drops a bracelet into a cave that supposedly contains a dangerous creature. Her curiosity implores her to enter, and what she finds turns her quest for a bracelet into a quest for truth.

AVAILABLE AT YOUR LOCAL COMICS SHOP OR BOOKSTORE! TO FIND A COMICS SHOP IN YOUR AREA, VISIT COMICSHOPLOCATOR.COM

For more information or to order direct: On the web: DarkHorse.com | Email: mailorder@darkhorse.com | Phone: 1-800-862-0052 Mon.–Fri. 9 a.m. to 5 p.m. Pacific Time

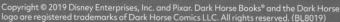